T0158159

Order this book online at www.trafford.com
email orders@trafford.com

Most Trafford titles are also available at major online book retailers.

Printed in the United States of America.

ISBN: 978-1-4669-0889-5 (sc)
ISBN: 978-1-4669-0890-1 (e)

Trafford rev. 12/22/2011

 www.trafford.com

North America & international
toll-free: 1 888 232 4444 (USA & Canada)
phone: 250 383 6864 ♦ fax: 812 355 4082

3012 A.D

REQUIEM OF AN EM

By
Timothy D. Eckert

Any work, without support from select stupendous individuals would never make its way into existence in the literary world. No backing of a work's conceiver would greatly reduce the number of writers throughout history. This book is no different.

The many thousands of hours spent trying to visualize this utopia would have been much harder to envisage had it not been for the many people that have been there to make my own life just as pleasant in reality as it would be in the coming fictional setting.

Looking back, the idea of this story would have first been toyed around with in high school when the young sophomores and I were presented to the true nature of current global affairs at the time, as well as other foundation-shaking concepts, such as existentialism, economics and college entrance exams. All of which called for each of us to think deeply about our lives, our futures and our existences to find out what we truly believe and want.

Out of this Great Period of Overthinking every detail of life is when I discovered that my best thoughts were the ones that were written out rather than spoken. Assisting me inspirationally in the academic world were some of the teachers that went above and beyond school policy to teach their students. To Mr. Bill Jones, my 7th grade ancient history teacher that inspired me to become a history teacher when I grew up. To Mr. Nicholas DeRosa, my sociology teacher who taught me all about human nature and gave me the insight on many cultural aspects about the human race. To Ms. Margaret Woodcock, my world history teacher who inspired me to dig deeper into my historical and sociological studies. To Dr. Onek Adyanga, one of my most favorite college professors and authors to date, Dr. Adyanga taught me one of the most valuable lessons of learning from history today to make tomorrow paradise. To all of these extraordinary people, this book is a testimony to all their hard work and of which I am forever grateful.

Furthermore, the support from all my friends, loving parents, brothers and others kept the momentum of the book in motion. A gracious thank you to all that have contributed to make this story possible. In full confidence I can truly say that I could have never done it without you . . .

—Timothy

"The world is a book, and those who
do not travel read only a page . . ."
—*St. Augustine*

For Hannah

PROLOGUE

The world. Well, it has not changed much in one thousand years. After all one cannot expect it to be too much different. The Middle Ages are not so very different from the year 2012. People in the Medieval times still farmed and wore clothes and had businesses with power hungry, land-grabbing rulers. They had taxes, families, religions, criminals and the same hills, fields and oceans we look over today. But here in the new current era, there are a few differences.

Oil is down to but a few small lakes beneath the desert sands and nuclear fusion and reaction is proving to be more costly than that of a person's weight in gold. Solar power has been the leading energy, until recently where certain minerals and rocks on none other than our very own orbiting Luna, can be reactive in a miracle process called Crystallic Fusion. The mixture of these moon minerals and rocks that are fused is called Lunex. The minerals can be installed in any device and are replaced tri monthly because the ionization transfer does not last for ever and the rocks become neutral or in a sense 'dead'; kind of like a battery.

The fusion is considered a God-sent miracle; the abundance of it just below the moon's surface makes it acquirable to even the most poverty stricken corners of the planet.

Technology has made a leap in humanity's existence. The hologram has been invented and perfected. Vehicles move on ball bearings rather than wheels. Military crafts the size of city blocks patrol the skies and space above countries, and if you possess the wealth for it, you can have a microscopic chip implanted in your head that receives signals and frequencies, so that you can listen to things such as your favorite songs or the latest headline news right in your very own cranium. This hasn't caught on yet with the average population but the projected sales outlook is good. What is common in just about every house though is your very own mechanical servant, or 'robot,' if you will. Simple machines that carry out the various burdensome tasks of the day.

In the world of politics there are only a couple of countries. Most of them are empires and almost all are continent sized. It would appear that the democratic trend of the third millennium A.D. began to show signs of slowing towards the latter half. More borders means more enemies and when oil and natural gas began to dry up, most countries were practically begging for a parental Motherland to watch over them by 2500 Current Era. Let's start with Europe . . .

Britain is once again an absolute monarchy with dominance over all the British Isles excluding Ireland as a whole and a protectorate over Australia, New Zealand, Tasmania, scattered regions throughout Africa and a few islands in the East Indies. King Geoffrey is the regal leader of this proud nation. With Britain's powerful navy, he is eager to stake a claim on his kingdom's former colonies . . .

As for fascist and ultra nationalist Germany, it controls all of Western Europe from the tip of Portugal to the borders of Poland, excluding Italy. This dominion was not given to Germany by consent of Europe either. Its leader is High Chancellor Warenhari Zeithen, who has modeled himself after one of the most sinister autobiographies in the history of civilization, Hitler's *Mein Kampf.* He splendors in putting labor camps back into the lives Europeans, and preforming mass public executions, controlling every aspect of the average citizen's life in order create the "Ultimate State." He is now on a political and religious vendetta against Europe for exploiting Germany's vast resources over the centuries and for Europe's weakness in dealing with surges of Muslim immigration and terrorism over the years. He is the Reich's self proclaimed, "steady hand at the Helm of Stability."

Russia concluded that democracy wasn't working to the government's benefit so they reverted to old-time Soviet communism around the year 2873, creating a neo-Bolshevik society. They now call their country Bolshevikvia in honor of the political party that first brought communism to the Motherland. Their Premier is "Fellow Comrade" Vladimir Boris Nevski. He too is a dictator that has longed for war with the rest of the world. Nevski was always under the notion that, "A country not at war is a country not worthy of being on the map." With his capital in Saint Petersburg, Bolshevikvia's western front has been ravaged and devastated at the wrath of Zeithen's Elite Juggernaut Forces. Russia has reclaimed all of its old republics that it had let go in the past and had previous influence on. These include Old Soviet Central Asia, Ukraine, Moldova, Belarus, Lithuania, Latvia,

Estonia, and Georgia. They have also extended their parental love to a few more regions including all of the Scandinavian countries, Poland, Old Czechoslovakia, Romania, The Balkans, Mongolia, Old Manchuria, Afghanistan, Pakistan and Alaska.

The entire Middle East has been secluded from the rest of the world. The U.N. simply decided, in 2907, that the Middle East was just too much of a burden for the rest of the world to deal with and that its problems should not have to reside on the shoulders of the rest of the global community. Too many countries in the region have their own people butchering each other just because their version of Islam is considered superior to that of rival ideals. Jihad is something that the world didn't want to deal with any longer. These quarrels are not limited to citizens of religions not native to the Middle East. The Jihad that was being carried out by Islamic fundamentalists is considered by the rest of the world to be ridiculous, barbaric and inhumane. It was decided after much debate and upheaval by the United Nations representatives that a militarized border be created by all neighboring nations to the Middle East. Naturally, Russia and Germany jumped at the opportunity and used the mandate to justify their otherwise genocidal ethnic cleansing of Muslims in Europe. They claimed that the mass killings were a result of illegal border crossing, regardless of how long they had resided in Europe. The entire enclosed region is known as the Middle Eastern Union or M.E.U. (The U.N. gave it this name in order to affirm a type of peace effort and unity for the quarrelsome countries.) Many felt angry that the acts of these fundamentalists were representing the Muslim world but the U.N. was simply fed up with the rise in terrorism in the past three hundred years. The M.E.U. region is divided into three provinces. The region that was once the Ottoman Empire over a thousand years ago is now the Ottoman province, the Arabian Peninsula is Arabia and all land to the east is Persia. No one is allowed in or out of this regional quarantine without proper authority by the U.N. and his or her own home country. The M.E.U. is allowed to trade with other countries for food and other necessities but no emigration is allowed. Egypt, Israel, the countries of North Africa, Central Asia, Albania and Bosnia are not included in M.E.U.

The Far East entered into one, large, united empire with their Japanese born Emperor, Ito Yokomoto. In 3006 Chancellor Zeithen presumed that Germany would not be able to win its war on Islam if the riches of the pagan East weren't acquired for the war effort. China in particular would provide a huge gateway of resources to the West. In 3007, he invaded China and Southeast Asia. His campaign was successful and soon all that was left was Japan and Indonesia. In the weeks before Chancellor Zeithen "extended his love" to Japan, Emperor Ito Yokomoto sent an urgent message to China and all southeast countries asking that they put aside their differences and unify. If they did not join together, Germany would surely control them all within a matter of months or even weeks. Since all the countries' leaders had already been sent back to Germany for public executions, he aired it on all radio, television and holo frequencies and channels. The people swiftly rose above through guerilla warfare and within a matter of months, Zeithen left Southeast Asia. The entire Far East regarded Yokomoto as a hero for his brilliant military coordination and mass guerilla invasions on Prussian army headquarters in China, Laos and Nepal. The liberated Asian countries felt that without Ito as Emperor, they would never survive another Western campaign and would be swept into the abyss of history. In 3009, he was given annexation privileges by all nations of the East Asia and Southeast Asia in turn that all the nations' leaders would become his Imperial viceroys on the mainland or at least have representatives in his Imperial Court.

Now most of Africa is claimed by the U.S. or R.N.A. (Republic of North America). The U.S. changed its name in 2662 after it economically acquired Mexico. Though the R.N.A. is Africa's current authoritative figure, they do not bother with Africa's poverty, ethnic unrest, or political issues. They are only there for the economic benefits and natural resources. Though at the beginning of American arrival, they offered food and medicine in return for minerals and precious metals, the flow of aid eventually slowed to a trickle and then stopped but exports continued to flow from West Africa to the U.S.

The current president of the R.N.A. is Alexandra Flinn who is considered to be one of the most ruthless American presidents of all time. She has already long over stayed her two terms in office by about three more terms. The R.N.A. is considered to be one of the greediest and most untrustworthy nations among the rest of the world. The U.K.'s King Geoffrey has organized many Pan-Africanism revolts to spite America, harboring an old grudge that America broke away from the British Empire eons ago. Currently the R.N.A. is composed of America, Mexico, Guatemala and the anarchist regions of West Africa.

America is a sad, hollow shell of what it used to represent in the year 3012. With Africa as its only bloodline, poorly resourced states in the Republic of North America are constantly threatening to leave the Union, preferring to chance sovereignty versus being starved by the Federal government. Along with it's collapsing economic state, militarily and technologically, the nation is actually regressing and has pretty much lost its any edge it used to have on the global community. In 2813, a deadly pandemic broke out in the western half of the country that later became known as the 'Cow Flu' and resulted in hundreds of millions of deaths. The worst plague in recorded history. As a result, natural elements such as forests and wild life began to grow again when the masses died out. More water collects in the deserts in the Southwest for cities to use. America in short has a new potential, resource wise, but now sadly is too backwards to take advantage of it any more.

Central America, not to mention just about all of South America, has given in to Colombo-Venezuelan invasion. A malevolent, military junta leader named General Alejandro Guamez operates the region. In 2994 he seized the capital of Colombia in an attempt to rid the country of its 'do little' president and regain glory for Colombia. After he 'alleviated' the president of his of his duties, he forced congress to disband as well as the remaining political representatives and politicians. Soon after, military leaders in Venezuela and Argentina followed suit in the junta revolution. His rule has left South and Central America in shambles as he has no control over drug lords, crime syndicates, and mafias all over the continent. Central and South America are considered to be as poor if not poorer than Africa and Southeast Asia.

A few other countries remain such as Ireland, the West Indies, India, Canada, a few nations in Africa and Iceland, that have not been affected by the rest of the globe's trend, but the rest have in a sense, "eaten or been eaten."

One more landmass exists that has only recently entered into the global community's politics as of the past three hundred years. It is called the Pacific Empire or Pacifica, often considered the Atlantis of the Pacific. In the year 2745, seismic activity of extraordinary proportion propelled a new landmass the size of Australia out into the Pacific Ocean. Since it was located literally right underneath the Hawaiian Islands, it was claimed promptly by the R.N.A. and was renamed Pacifica. The R.N.A. built its largest military harbor there, calling it Wellington's Harbor after the grand admiral who had organized its construction. They made it their primary naval base mainly because it was the closest national defense position against Bolshevikvia. In 2897, the R.N.A. intercepted a holo message from Bolshevikvia to Germany boasting that the Red Army was going to launch the greatest invasion on the R.N.A. since the past eleven hundred years when Germany invaded all of Europe during World War II. Recognizing that no fuel had arrived at the harbor in the past year for the super freighters and aircraft carriers due to the deteriorating economy, the R.N.A. panicked. In fact, half of the vessels docked there were completely empty. The R.N.A. made a cowardly move and withdrew all military units, sending them back to the naval bases in Nevada and the island of California, and abandoned all the state's civilians to face the imminent Bolshevik attack. Twelve hours before the Reds invaded, Germany made a traitorous and foolish move thinking that the troops and air forces had already left or were leaving. German troops moved into Moscow, Odessa, Kiev, Minsk, and Stockholm. Much to their disdain, Communist forces had not left and were able to repel the Germanic invaders at a costly victory. Too costly to attack Pacifica. When the island realized what had almost happened to them, they were outraged that the R.N.A. abandoned them and demanded independence from the R.N.A., wanting to become their own nation. Fearful that the U.N. would place further sanctions or trade embargoes on the R.N.A. for their insufficient and inability to maintain and protect the own borders and abandoning an entire state, in 2898, the R.N.A. granted Pacifica independence.

Its first ruler ever was the original R.N.A. governor named Edward Augustus. He was born and raised on the island so he naturally knew what the people needed and wanted. When he was voted into office for governor it was a 98 percent to 2 percent landslide of a win, so naturally the public looked to him to be their first independent leader. It was decided by the population that democracy was too unreliable, did not work to the people's benefits, takes forever to get something accomplished and makes it simple for a corrupt politician to get a rise to power. So it was decided that the island would be ruled by a monarchy with a royal family and a minor parliament that would keep watch over the royal family's jurisdiction.

Though they do not resemble it, the royal family has roots that go back to northern Italy; consequently Pacifica's only main religion is Roman Catholicism. Eastern Orthodoxy is accepted and the island's native Polynesian minorities are also allowed to continue their traditions. Protestantism is strictly outlawed, proclaimed by lawmakers that it would cause civil unrest among citizens. Emperor Edward had a palace built in the capital city of New Rome where most of the country's affairs take place. Edward was notorious for his love of history. One of his goals was to model Pacifica after the Romans in architecture, laws and traditions. He had a complete functional replica of the Colosseum built in New Rome in dedication to Neptune whom his Roman ancestors had worshipped in the past. In addition, he built a Catholic cathedral that rivals that of Notre Dame. His other goal was to convert the nation's language from English to Latin. He succeeded in both before he died.

Now, over one hundred years later, the heir is the twenty-eight year old great-great grandson named Charles and a young former Grand Duchess now married to Crowned Prince Charles named Octavia. The entire National Cathedral in the city of New Rome is filled to its limits with awe filled spectators as they watch the Pope prepare the coronation of their new Emperor and Empress . . .

CANTO I

As the Pope waved incense around the alter, Charles and Octavia knelt on both knees on the white marble steps in front. An anxious aura hung in the cool cathedral. Mass had just ended, along with all the homilies that many Pacifican officials and clerics had to offer on the coronation. The ceiling and walls were vibrantly painted with angels and saints in the clouds, images depicting heaven and Mary along with Jesus in her arms. Along all the sides were marble carved head busts of famous Popes, Saints and Apostles from ages ago. On the right side of the cathedral, choirs sang joyous chants and the symphonies played Roman styled fanfares. Charles felt his knees and shins start to fall asleep but there was nothing he could do. He was fixated in a position with his thighs and back straight, his head aimed down at the floor. His right hand was in a fist and was positioned across his chest and directly over his heart. He held in the crook of his left arm a gold and red-feathered centurion helmet that represents his position in royalty as Crowned Prince. He donned a white suit-type dress coat with a red underdress shirt and white suit pants. A dark gray cape hung over his left shoulder along with matching dark gray gloves on both hands. Metals, pins and awards hung over both sides of his front suit jacket. Charles is a striking man around five feet, eleven inches. He has light brown, almost dirty blonde, hair and dark blue eyes. Typically, royal heirs so young as Charles aren't crowned so early in life but because his father was untimely shot down over German airspace, he had to assume the throne within the year.

Octavia was to his right in a white silk dress with a long cape, made with white lilies and palm leaves. She too had her head bowed to the floor. She held both of her hands in a praying position just below her face against her chest. Around her neck she wore multiple strings of pearls and had a pair of gold earrings on her ears. Octavia was graced with long, dark brown wavy hair and very light blue eyes. She felt increasingly uneasy as she noticed out of the corner of her eye that the entire crowd was staring at her. She never liked public appearances but it was part of the regal position. The Pope finished and handed the incense to a bishop, then turned to the congregation of spectators.

"My fellow brothers and sisters, we come here today before Almighty God in this cathedral to witness the coronation and consecration of the Crowned Prince, Charles Simon Augustus and the Grand Duchess, Octavia Elizabeta Augustus." He turned to Octavia first. The Pope held in his right hand a golden staff with the crucifix at the top. "Octavia Elizabeta, do you solemnly swear by your soul and heart that you shall uphold and lead this empire with a just and compassionate hand? That you will put the burdens of the empire in your hands for the good and welfare of the people? Do you swear?" As he asked her, he tapped both her shoulders, then her forehead.

"I do."

He then turned and took a silver container from a bishop, dipped a finger into the oils and made the sign of the cross on Octavia's forehead. "Octavia Elizabeta," he paused then took an olive branch crown made of silver from a cardinal and slowly placed it on her head, "I crown thee the royal Empress of Pacifica." The cathedral erupted in cheering and shouting of, "All hail Octavia!" She felt exhilarated. Her hands trembled with joy. The Pope raised his arms and the cathedral became completely silent again. He now turned to Charles. Pope Marcus XXIII slowly withdrew a sword from Charles' sheath. It was the same one that was made by Edward the Great and passed down to each emperor. It had a gold hilt and a silver blade with a button on the hilt that could open the sword into a trident. He repeated the same process. "Charles Simon, do you solemnly swear by your soul and heart that you shall rule the empire with a just and firm hand? That you will rule this beautiful and holy land with the same laws that the Almighty Lord gave to Moses thousands of years before us? That you will carry burdens of this nation on your shoulder to lead this empire according to what the Lord wishes to complete in this world? Do you swear?"

"I swear, Your Holiness."

The Pope then put oil on his head and placed the sword back into the sheath. He then took a golden crown of olive branches from another cardinal. Charles could feel his face flush red. He felt jittery with excitement. "Charles Simon, Prince of Pacifica, I crown thee the royal Emperor of the Pacific Empire. Go forth and lead this land to further the glory of God the Father." The Pope stepped back and made the sign of the cross in front of them. "In nomine Patris, et Filii, et Spiritus Sancti. Amen. Pacifica, I am pleased to present to you your new Emperor and Empress!"

"They have bigger things to worry about."

Edward Palace sat somewhat hidden in a large, tropical plot of land positioned in the very center of New Rome. From inside the property, one would never be able to tell that they were in the center of the metropolis. Colossal palms and dense jungle fauna smothered out any view of the city and its skyscrapers. They pulled in at the marble steps of the palace and four guards stood in front. Statues of his great great grandfather Edward, Caesar, Neptune, and Saint Paul the Apostle were in various places in front of the palace. Charles took Octavia's hand and escorted her out of the limo.

A centurion stepped in front of them. "Your majesties, welcome to Edward Palace." They nodded and started up the steps . . .

CANTO II

The inside of Edward Palace was almost all but fantasy. Octavia's eyes twinkled in awe as they wandered inside their new royal home. Red and gold carpets covered the floors and hand carved marble pillars held the ceiling above. In the west wing, a room three stories tall, was where all the dinner parties were held. The entire west wall was one solid plate of glass that overlooked the Imperial gardens. A statue of Neptune on a dolphin-pulled chariot was in the center of the room with fountains at the base. Chefs and servants bustled around the room with trays of decorations and flowers.

They continued down the corridor. In the parliamentary wing, there was a large marble room that held a large black slate table lined with gold trimmings and the olive crown emblem in the center. All along the walls of parliament were computer panels that showed various places of the world. Some were concentrated on certain sections of the island. Others were on Bolshevikvia and Germany. Warrenhari's profile was on one and Alexandra Flinn's was on another.

"I guess parliament will be indulging us in this tomorrow on such affairs," said Charles.

"Oh. Splendid."

They continued through the palace to a room that served the same purpose as the oval office would in the White House. It was a large room with Greek-style marble pillars and red velvet carpet. It had maps of the empire hanging on the wall and painted murals of famous historical events such as the Pope first arriving in Pacifica and the christening by Emperor Scipio of the two largest naval ships ever built. They were anointed the Leviathan and the Kraken. These two mythical creatures were originally the guardian of Atlantis and the terror of the Northern Atlantic seas. Sailors from every nation in ancient times would wet themselves at the notion of running into these monsters. It was only fitting that these imposing and destructive ships be named as such. Another mural was of Romulus Augustus, the last Roman emperor no more than 15 years of age, looking out over the balcony of his palace as the Germans sacked the capital city with Odoacer, the German Chieftain, riding on a black horse directly towards the palace. The last mural depicted was not of historical record but what every Pacifican hoped and prayed for every night and before every meal. It showed the Emperor of Pacifica (not any in particular because the face is hazy) seated at a long table during a feast. Seated at his sides were the premier of the Supreme Union of Soviet Bolsheviks conversing with a Pope and shaking hands regarding a union between fellow Catholics and the Eastern Orthodox Church. The other side depicted the high chancellor of Germany (his face also hazy because frankly nobody knows when this would ever occur) laughing with an emperor of Eastern Asia. It was the picture perfect symbol of peace. All of Pacifica's enemies dining in perfect harmony with the Emperor and his allies. Charles smiled.

"Hmm. Beautiful but . . . unrealistic."

She sighed. "It'll be difficult but I wouldn't rule it out. Nothing is impossible, Charles," said Octavia.

"Its a little hard to practice peaceful counter action against Bolshevik warheads aimed right at where we stand right now."

"Well, like I said. Anything is possible."

A door swung open and a tiny pitter-patter of footsteps preceded a little boy no older than four years old. He had short brown hair with a rosy face. His outfit was nearly identical to Charles' except it was missing the decorated awards and the crown.

"Father, I'm finished with saying my rosary at the monastery with the arch deacon. He says I'll soon be ready for my first studies," said the boy. Charles' son, Giuseppe, entered the room in a flurry. An intelligent boy for his age, he was more inquisitive about the world around him than his peers.

"Well that's wonderful. I'm glad to hear you're moving up in your academics."

"I like history the best," said the boy.

"Hmm. I too love history. You know what they say, 'He who does not learn history is condemned to repeat it.'"

"Really Father?"

"It's true. Take Napoleon. When he led his campaign into Russia during the winter, they were completely unprepared. Consequently, the French were stopped dead in their tracks because of the harsh Russian winter. Then about one hundred fifty years later, Adolf Hitler led his armies into the Soviet Union. They were actually doing well until winter came. Their tanks and machinery failed to work and soon after that the Soviets were able to drive the Germans away from Moscow. If Hitler would have paid attention in history class, he would have been smart and attacked in the summer."

"Wow, that's interesting."

"I know, and that's just one example. There's millions of other events similar to ones like that."

"Do you think the High Chancellor will be foolish enough to do the same?"

Charles laughed. "It would be to our advantage but I think he probably has it together this time around."

Charles stood in front of a large mirror while servants bustled around him making sure his suit was fitted to perfection. Others buzzed around Octavia's face and dress, arranging her hair and make-up and polishing her silver crown.

A short, impatient Polynesian man in a tuxedo approached one of the servants.

"How much longer? The Pope has just arrived as well as three of five expected Imperial Legion Generals."

A servant was pulling out the last of the curlers in Octavia's hair. "We'll be done in about 3 minutes."

"They need to be out there in one."

Octavia overheard him. "Oroiti, the Emperor and I will be attending the festival in three minutes."

He paused. Though he was taken aback he was in no position to say anything. He bowed to her and left. Charles finished and walked over to her. She looked at him with a cocked eyebrow. He rolled his eyes and leaned forward to whisper in her ear.

"It's our first day in Edward Palace. Lets try not to get all the servants to hate us so soon."

"They're *servants*. It's their job to *serve* us."

He sighed. The attendants finally finished with her hair and three Imperial guards came in to escort them out to the feast. In the west wing where the enormous ballroom was located, hundreds of dignitaries from all over the empire were cheering as the two descended the staircase towards their guests. Charles could see his life long friend, General Di'Orlo in front of them next to his son Giuseppe, and his daughter, Cipriana, who was just a few years older than her brother. He held up his hands and the cheering stopped.

"This day . . . does not belong to my wife or I alone, but to all citizens of the empire. This day marks another line in the sands of time of peaceful transition by holy coronation. Not through corrupt purchase. Not through a military coup. Not through faulty democracy or forced electoral votes. This age old monarchy is the Almighty Lord's gift to one of the corners of the world that still recognizes him as the divine architect of the universe. In these trying times . . . the patriotic loyalty you all portray is enough to bring a tear to my eye. This holy continent . . . waging our crusade on the evil tyranny and oppression that keeps this world from the Lord's goal of world peace and harmony for humanity. May God keep you all in the palm of his hand." As Charles and Octavia continued down the staircase to the feast, the cheering began to fill the ballroom again.

<u>CANTO III</u>

The following day at roughly noon, the Emperor sat in the parliamentary war room, listening to the daily briefing on the most current, secret and tactical information on the rest of the globe. Octavia was slouched in her chair, lost in her own thoughts. Charles, dismayed at the German advancement, sat at the front of the table with his arms plastered straight out and fingers spread wide apart. His head hung low as General Di'Orlo continued his debriefing on the enemies of the Empire.

He pointed up to one of the screens. "High Chancellor Zeithen was last seen in the south of France with his wife Hermia and his S.S. lieutenants Gustav and Gottschalk. As you can see here, the Germans have been pressing closer to the Alps." while red arrows indicating the German armies on the screen moving south presented a visual, "and are expected to make it across into Italy in a matter of days."

One of the members of parliament spoke up. "So I presume it is safe to say they will not heed our ultimatum we sent eight days ago. We need to hold up our end of the bargain. If they reach Rome, the homeland of our holy roots and of all Christianity will fall to those barbarians."

"I agree," said Di'Orlo.

"General, this may seem brash and I know that I am a just a member of parliament and not a man of military stance but, if our troops are ready when would be the earliest they could be dispatched? And where?"

"Sir, it's good that you said something because I brought all the documents required for such a dispatch of our troops." Charles raised his head and looked at the General, inquisitively. "I just need all the members of this parliament as well as Grand Admiral Mozzollio, and his Majesty to sign. King Geoffrey wishes to be informed if we take the initiative so that they can meet us in Iberia. They are currently holding their own in the English Channel. The British armada has been particularly keen on what sails off their shores." The parliament members whispered among themselves. They soon started to examine the dispatch permission documents.

Charles leaned back and silently moaned in dismay. This wasn't how he had intended his first day as emperor to be. Octavia leaned towards him. "Charles, it's been coming for a long time now. Your own father was shot down not too long ago because of these heathens. The sooner we initiate this, the sooner Europe can fend for itself."

"Octavia, wars last years. Sometimes decades. If the Empire jumps in, we'll have a bigger target on our backs than all of Europe itself."

"Charles, if we don't it may be you who gets shot down while accompanying a supply of food and weapons to Europe. It may be you who is laid in a sarcophagus next to his father's in a matter of weeks, for none other than the same exact reason!"

The Grand Admiral of the Imperial Air force, Mozzollio finished dotting his *i*'s and placed the manila folder neatly and squarely in front of the Emperor. He looked at his wife. She gazed back into his eyes for a few moments, and then slowly nodded her head up and down once. He looked back at the folder then opened it. Inside was one sheet of paper. At the top it stated,

Operation Overview;

By ordinance of the Imperial government of the Pacific Empire, VIII legions of all branches of the Holy Army, Navy, and Air/Orbital forces are to be dispatched to the Iberian Peninsula, and with the help of the British, assist the kingdom of Spain in repelling the German forces across the Pyrenees Mountains. From there, Pacifica is to create a blockade at the Pyrenees Mountains to prevent German forces from crossing into Spain; thus making a tactical foothold for Pacifica and its allies.

He looked up at General Di'Orlo. "Why the Pyrenees? I thought we were discussing Italy?"

"If we help Spain and Portugal, much of Zeithen's armies that are at the Alps will double back and head directly for the Pyrenees range. The large division in the German army should allow for Italy to hold their defenses by themselves without risk of breach. If we were to land in Italy, we would have to overcome the German navy in the Mediterranean *and* if we did make it there in one piece, the swell of German forces pouring into Italy would be near invincible. This is the best possible tactic."

Charles slowly removed a pen from his breast pocket. Everyone in the parliament room anxiously stared at him. For a brief moment he felt as if the weight of the world was on his shoulders. He felt almost immature for so quickly signing off on a declaration of war on his second day. He then remembered all the images he had seen on the news and in briefings, horrible images. People being herded like beasts into compounds and installations. People starving, clothing literally falling from their backs. He brooded on what the world would be like if all corners of the earth had similar sights like this. He could never forgive himself if anything like that ever hit his empire. It was his duty as emperor. He dipped his pen in a vile of ink and signed his name.

Octavia gave a faint smile. Charles then took the paper and placed it in a little press. He pressed it down, then back up. It now had a raised emblem on it of the Imperial seal. He placed the paper back in the manila folder as neatly as he had found it. He closed it and handed the folder to General Di'Orlo. He looked up at him. "Assemble the legions."

The parliament room exploded into shouting and cheering. General Di'Orlo swiftly placed his fist over his heart, extended it straight out, then briskly walked out.

As the sun began to set on the palms of the Imperial Garden, Charles sat at his desk in his personal study with his son, Giuseppe, tutoring him on the ages of old. Though the heir was young, his mind was more inquisitive than any child that Charles could ever think of, never placing any bounds or limits on knowledge. Charles asked him another question.

"How many of King Leonidas' soldiers were sent from Sparta to fight King Darius' armies of Persia?"

"Three hundred, I believe."

"Very good! But why did Persia invade?"

"Sparta had helped Ionia in a revolt against the Persians a decade before."

"Excellent. You know, my son, the Ottoman province is, in a sense, a graveyard of empires and kingdoms. I'd say roughly five thousand years ago, the Hittites set up a relatively expansive kingdom. They were constantly quarreling with the Egyptians over the lands between them. As a result the Israelites were always caught in the middle. Later, Greeks who began calling the area 'Ionia' settled the northern coastal tip. They founded the famous city-state of Troy. It wasn't long before it succumbed to Persian rule. Later, as the Persian Empire began to crumble and fall apart, the Romans quickly moved in. After the western half of the Roman Empire fell to the German tribes, the eastern half came under the rule of Byzantium. It went on to reclaim the remnants of Old Rome under Justinian around five fifty A.D. It too finally fell in the fourteen hundreds to the Ottomans. The Ottoman Empire went on to take all the lands that Byzantium originally had. After World War one, the allied forces of Europe carved up the Ottoman Empire into many countries, the biggest being Turkey. It finally ends a few hundred years ago when the U.N. unified the Middle East, making the Anatolian peninsula of Turkey into the Ottoman Provence."

Charles leaned back in his seat and smiled at his baffled son. Giuseppe stared into space for a moment, trying to process all the ancient history. After a few moments, he met eyes with his father. "It seems as if most of the world's great empires were founded on peninsulas or islands."

"That is very observant of you and it's true. If there is more water covering the borders, the chance of attack is less *and* it is much easier to ward off an army that is still trying to land on the shore. Its not like the ships have anywhere to go if they are on fire. Yes indeed, the Greeks, Romans, Mayans, Ottomans, Minoans, Arabians, the Spanish, the Vikings, Britons, Swedes, Japanese-they all were geographically blessed with . . . none other than . . . water."

"Swedes?" asked Giuseppe.

Charles laughed. "The Swedes didn't always make lavish furniture for the world. There was a time when Sweden possessed the most feared warriors in all of Europe.

"Interesting."

"Here's another one for you. What special day in the Roman calendar was Julius Caesar murdered on?"

"The Ides of March."

"Good. What day is the Ides of March?"

"The seventeenth?"

"Close, the fifteenth. Alexander the Great of Macedonia introduced Greek culture to the Persian lands that he attained. This brought about a short but unique era called the what?"

"The Hellenistic era."

"Excellent!" Charles smiled at his son, dumbfounded by his expansive knowledge.

"Confucius taught lessons in ancient China and they were kept in a collective book called the analects. They told of how citizens and rulers all had a duty to serve one another and how to live a prosperous life. What was an aspect of his teachings that was missing?"

"Well, they didn't tell of any after life or what should be done to achieve it."

He paused, thinking of a final question. "Last question, what is . . . forty eight divided by eight?"

"Hmm. Four?"

"No, the answer is six. That's quite all right though, mathematics is one aspect of academics that takes years of practice."

"Father, I don't like math. Not at all," Giuseppe said outright.

"Do you want to hear a little secret of mine?" asked Charles. Giuseppe eagerly nodded his head and leaned closer in Charles' face. "I absolutely loath mathematics. That's why I leave it to the stock markets traders."

Giuseppe giggled. "You're funny, father."

Charles smiled at him. "You'll make a great emperor someday. Hmm. Well, I guess that's enough tutoring for today."

"Father, why is the world so confusing?"

"Well, my son, we've been around for many thousands of years and—."

"I mean like now. In other countries, like in America and Europe."

Charles paused thinking of how to answer his child without alarming him. "We'll, it's been a long time since God has sent anyone to set us straight. People's values diminish over time. They're just out for themselves. In America, the concept of democracy and all the rights and amendments that are installed have led people to believe that anything that infringes on their rights is bad, even when it is our own Divine Almighty telling them not to do something. They can't seem to understand that the world doesn't revolve around them. All they care about is their 'rights'. It is a selfish way of thinking. The 'right' to religious freedom has led to the absence of Christ in the classroom or the courts." All these 'rights' are not doing anyone justice at all. It's unbelievable that they wonder why all their children are nothing but little juvenile delinquents. Did you know that it is illegal in America to spank a child when the child has misbehaved?"

"If they don't spank or slap then how do they get the child to behave, father?"

"I've been contemplating the same question myself."

"You know what they say, spare the rod, spoil the child," said Octavia as she walked into the study.

Charles looked up at her. "He's coming along quite remarkably. I'm very impressed," he said.

She smiled. "I knew he would. Giuseppe sweetheart, General Di'Orlo's nephew, Vincent is waiting for you in the lobby downstairs." At the news, Giuseppe got up and hurried out of Charles' large study.

Charles looked at her. "I think I am going to write an Emperor Proclamation."

"Already? It's only been a day," she said in surprise. An Emperor Proclamation was a letter to the Empire stating what the Emperor's goals were during his reign and what he was expecting of his citizens. Usually they called for special attention to prayer, obedience, or education.

"This world . . . hasn't had a prophet since our Lord ascended. There have been saints and martyrs, but no one to set the code of conduct . . . how to go about the world. Europe, until Germany expanded, was on a religious decline. Not that they don't believe, its just that since they have swung into a socialist trend, the government takes such good care of them that they don't feel obliged anymore. Let's face it; this world is a sad little place to live. I want to make it absolutely clear that I will never allow these primitive, prehistoric human impulses to ever be acceptable in this empire. It's emotions like this that got Adam and Eve kicked out of the Garden of Eden. This empire . . . this island, is our second chance at innocence and fulfillment."

"Well, if you feel you are ready, than by all means I encourage you. Have you been reflecting on this for a while now?"

"Actually, no. I only thought about it today when Giuseppe asked sort of a general question about the world. It really got me thinking."

"Well, in that case I don't want to disrupt your train of thought. I just wanted to see how you and Giuseppe were coming along. Oh, by the way, the head clerics from the monastery from the west side of New Rome will be here after dinner to discuss funding for more dormitories for the monks."

"By head clerics, you mean?" he asked.

"The Abbot and the Archdeacon, and . . . a couple of administrative friars and monks."

"Oh yes, I believe now that the Abbot sent me a holo before Giuseppe came in for his studies, that's right."

Octavia smiled at him. Then, she turned and left silently. Charles turned back to his desk and pulled up his holo screen and thought about what he had explained to Giuseppe a few minutes prior, then began typing furiously.

> To my beloved citizens of the Empire of the Pacific, peace be unto you. I come to you all with my earnest and holy request. The world is eroding beneath our feet and the fundamental elements of a Judaic-Christian society are fading into the abyss amidst human progression . . ."

The words poured from his fingers like water. He thoughts flowed in syncracy inside his head. He soon would have an outline for the Pacificans to follow designed to achieve peace and harmony, while preserving the archaic traditions and laws of old.

Charles walked out onto the Imperial Gardens into a large trellis covered in beautiful jungle fauna and vines, still tasting his Tilapia from dinner, where an Abbot and his fellow clerics from the monastery sat patiently. They stood up as he approached them and then slightly bowed. He lifted his hand to them and then lowered it. The Abbot spoke up. "Your Majesty, I am Abbott Barrone, head of the St. Clement monastery in the farthest end of western New Rome. These are my fellow monks, friars, and deacons. It is a bucolic little sanctuary where clerics alike come to perform to the full obligation of committing themselves to God. That is why we have come before you today. As you can imagine, with the increase in youth joining the clergy, our holy haven has become a little crowded as far as living space. Our libraries and studies have also become a little small and the students frequently have to wait awhile just to further their studies. The monastery is a little past two hundred years old. We want to keep the original sandstone architecture while updating living quarters and other necessities. We wanted to ensure that this problem wouldn't happen anytime soon so we have a financial estimate plan for the sanctuary." The Abbot handed a sheet that had the financial estimate on it.

"Of course. I think that it is a splendid idea that you have taken the initiative to expand the monastery. Pardon me for asking, but isn't this under the Diocesan Jurisdiction?"

"Well your Majesty, we did go to the Bishop but he felt that 1.7 million natos was a tad to high for renovations but he said that we should approach you before dipping into the funds of the Diocese considering the royal family is one of the Church's biggest contributors [one imperial nato is worth the roughly same as two American dollars]."

"Well then, in light of that you have my blessing to commence on this reconstruction of the monastery. I don't see anything conflicting with those numbers or requests. How many students do you have currently?"

"We have a little over one hundred and ten but we had roughly 60 other applicants that were unable to attend because of there being no room in the sanctuary. Those numbers will probably increase within a few years," said the Archdeacon, next to the Abbot.

"Goodness. I applaud you, Abbot Barrone, for taking the initiative for this. Yes you can tell the Bishop that you and the Archdeacon have the Emperor's consent."

"Thank you, your Majesty. God be with you on your quest to Iberia. We understand that you will be leaving tomorrow evening to Britannia. We will praying for you and the Empire." The Abbot extended his hand and Charles kissed it. He then stepped back and bowed to Charles.

"Thank you, brothers," said the Emperor. They turned and silently walked away and out of the gardens. Charles remained on the marble bench, watching the last of the sun set over the palms.

CANTO IV

Charles stood on the command deck of the space plane, *HMS The Penitent,* overlooking the foggy North Atlantic. The command deck was a glass dome on the underside of the ship with many levels to overlook a battlefield from the air. On its left and right side, the space plane was accompanied by the *HMS Juggernaut* and the *HMS Promethium*. A stark woman's voice came over the vessel's intercom, "We are approaching the western Irish Coast. Estimated time to London is one hour." Grand Admiral Mozzollio walked over to Charles and bowed to him.

"Your Majesty, I thought that I should give you your next twenty four hour schedule now that we are nearing the British Isles. When we arrive in London, the King of England will be awaiting your arrival. After we arrive, he wishes that you would accompany him back to Buckingham Palace for dinner and afternoon festivities. In the evening, the Archbishop of Canterbury wishes to talk to you concerning our Church and the Anglican Church. Tomorrow, Parliament has arranged to meet with you,

General Di'Orlo, myself and one of our head parliamentary members Alfonso Fulgenetti."

"Thank you, Grand Admiral." Charles nodded his head and Mozzollio bowed down low to him.

Something started to repeatedly ricochet off the glass from below.

"What is that?" Startled, they both looked down at the ocean. In between patches of fog, they could make out a tiny assault ship speeding for its life across the waves being pursued by two British battle cruisers.

"Germans, your Majesty. Spiteful little bastards if you don't mind me saying." Moments later, precautionary alarms sounded. A decorated officer approached the Grand Admiral.

"Sir, we're picking up benign fire from a German assault ship. Do you wish to aid the English navy in the engagement?"

"No. Remain on the scheduled course, Captain."

"Yes sir." The captain walked over to a command desk and picked up the intercom. "All staff are to report back to their appointed stations."

Mozzollio turned back to the Emperor. "I don't believe that will be the only resistance that we will face, your majesty. But something so minuscule as a lone assault ship is not even worth our attention. What is important is that you arrive in London in a little less than an hour along with the general and I."

King Geoffrey stood accompanied by royal grenadiers on all sides at the landing pad at the Morcaster Military Instillation in London. Behind them was an enormous array of soldiers, parliament members, generals, admirals, lieutenants, field marshals, diplomats and bureaucrats alike standing in an orderly fashion, facing each other from across a purple velvet carpet. He felt his cape and crown begin to blow around as the one hundred foot long propellers that held the space plane in the air began to near the ground. The King had never gotten this close to one of the planes and guessed that the *HMS The Penitent* must be around the size of three or four city blocks. The hum of the engines was deafening but soon died down when the stabilizers extended and a ramp lowered from the belly of vessel.

King Geoffrey, like Charles, was also young. He had red hair and a short red beard, which made his Irish ancestry quite prevalent. He wore a traditional purple and white furred robe, though not as gaudy as a monarch would during the Renaissance. His crown was golden and had four jewel arches that intersected over his cranium with a cross at the top. The inside was lined with purple velvet and gold lining.

Geoffrey too had lost his father at a young age but to a brain tumor rather than crashing down to earth in a fiery inferno like Charles' father. He and his uncle had contended for four years after for the crown. His uncle had argued that Geoffrey was too young and Geoffrey argued that it was he who was the ruler and direct heir of the late king. In the end, Geoffrey of course had won but it was that event that Charles had given the nickname of 'Hamlet' to Geoffrey for his confrontation with his uncle.

When Charles began to descend the steps with the rest of the Pacifican officials, an orchestra began to play God Save the Queen while King Geoffrey started over to greet him. Charles put on an inviting grin at the site of seeing his old friend for the first time in what seemed like eons.

"Emperor Charles, I welcome you to Great Britain. Your arrival has been most anticipated by everyone in the whole of England."

Charles approached the king with a bright smile and gave him a bear hug. "I hope we did not keep you waiting very long now, Hamlet," he said with a smirk.

"Oh Charley, when have you ever been late?" said Geoffrey, rolling his eyes and laughing in the process. The two turned and began to walk down the purple carpet.

"So I hear from the imperial war ministry that you're in the mood for a bloody good assault against Zeithen and his neophyte Nazi Prussia, starting with Iberia, eh chap?"

"Well, that's the objective my friend, but I would bet it is easier said than done. That is why I have brought the heads of each branch of the Imperial Military to discuss operation plans although I'm almost certain that you should have received an operations summary no more than twenty-four hours ago."

"Why, yes indeed I did. My troops are assembling as we speak for departure from England. We just need to discuss specifics, times, and of course the exact place because after all Iberia is a big peninsula."

"I agree with you one hundred percent, Geoff," said Charles.

The king smiled. "But first, we must have dinner. My chefs have prepared roast goose for us. I don't want us thinking on empty stomachs." They continued into the instillation followed by the rest of the king's welcome wagon while the two escort space planes began landing as well . . .

In the main dining hall in Buckingham Palace, General Di'Orlo noticed that the sky was growing from gray to darker gray as he passed around the final documentation to be signed by the King and by England's finest military heads. He, like Charles, was stuffed from the roast goose dinner and did not have the luxury of reclining back in the soft padded chairs in the room. One of the more dim members of the British parliament raised his hand.

"So, how are we going to meet up in the Atlantic and make our way to Spain without the Germans catching wind of our little surprise play date with them?"

General Di'Orlo internally groaned, then pointed back up at the holo screen at the front of the room, but Grand Admiral Mozzollio arose to clarify, relieving him. "The *HMS KRACKEN* is currently anchored off the coast of Iceland and a fourth of the Empire's Atlantic naval branch (Pacifica's Imperial navy is divided in half into two branches. The Atlantic branch and the Pacific branch) is currently in the North Atlantic Sea. Another third is out near the mid Atlantic ridge."

"As I'm sure you're aware, our ships regularly return to our continent to return our troops who have served their terms. Their scheduled terms are soon going to be exhausted and they *will* have to return and German intelligence is well aware of that. To fool them, we will have our ships in the North Atlantic, including the *KRAKEN,* make their way out to the mid Atlantic while the ships at the mid Atlantic ridge will make their way east towards the Mediterranean. Your navy off the coast of Mauritania will move up north. We will all meet in the Azores and plow full speed ahead to the Portugal coast, catching the Germans off guard. Until we make our way to the coast, it will all look like benign naval procedure to the Germans. That is why we must move at top speeds to get there. If we moved fast enough, we'll be anchored off Iberia in a little over forty-five minutes."

"What if we have missile opposition from their coastal headquarters?" asked the parliament member.

"The *KRAKEN's* missile defense system is state of the art and has proven its dependability multiple times on the high seas."

"I see. No more questions for me."

The *HMS KRAKEN* was a godlike ship that every nation held in fear. Allies and enemies always spoke of the ship with respect. Named after the creature in Norse mythology that would grab defenseless ships and drag them to the blue depths, the ship was almost impenetrable. Its hull was made of steel a foot thick and was the biggest naval vessel ever constructed making it one of the eighth man-made wonders of the world. It was seven times the size of an ocean liner and roughly the height of one of the former World Trade Center towers, making it almost impossible to dock anywhere. In fact, it was so large that it had a section just for manufacturing its own ammunition and rockets. Its vast targeting system and missile defense system made it impossible to drop anything onto it and was capable of holding half of the legions that were needed for Iberia. Since there were two in existence, its sister ship was known as the *HMS LEVIATHAN*. Both the Greeks and the Hebrews held the Leviathan in contempt. According to the Greeks, the Leviathan was the guardian of the gates to Atlantis. So it was fitting to the Emperor that one of these invincible ships guarding Pacifica be named so.

Di'Orlo stepped forward again with the signatures of everyone except the king. He bowed down to the ruler and placed it in front of him on the table. One of his advisers leaned in to his ear.

"We just need yours now, your highness."

The king took a fountain pen out from his pocket and signed anxiously. He put the pen down neatly on the table and the room filled up with cheering men throwing their arms up in the air and loud "huzzas."

Geoffrey put his hand in the air and the grand dining hall fell quiet. "The Emperor and I will now be out for good fox hunt. I believe you chaps have a lot to attend to

considering the time frame we are given. God save England."
With that just about everyone stood up and hustled out of
the room. He looked at Charles. "Come, we should make
our way to the stables before it gets too dark. Have you ever
been on the hunt before, Charley?"

"No, I don't believe I ever have."

"Well, I know you will enjoy this. It is best when the
forest is foggy anyway, never mind the weather."

Geoffrey stood up and turned to a servant. "Ready a
hunting outfit for Emperor Charles."

"Yes, your highness."

He got up and followed King Geoffrey out of the dining
hall.

In the late afternoon fog, Charles could barely make out
the forest's features in front of him and doubted the horse
that he was riding on could make them out either. About six
foxhounds stayed along side the King. The air was cool and
refreshing from the stuffy, hot air of Buckingham Palace.
The breeze was crisp against his skin. He and Geoffrey had
donned white pants, a red jacket and a black riding helmet.
Geoffrey pulled his horse back next to his.

"So Charley, I haven't even asked about your lovely
family. How is your wife and children?"

"I think they're adjusting very well to our new lives
as the Empire's royal family. Octavia certainly has been
enjoying the limelight lately."

"She'll make a fine empress, your wife will. I'm sure of
it."

"Yes, eventually she will settle down from all the
commotion of the coronation." He sighed quietly.

"When my wife Nora and I were crowned King and
Queen of England, I had second thoughts too about her
being in the spotlight of royalty."

"What do you mean?"

"What do I mean? Well, Charley, Nora just wasn't acting like a queen, and I was a little troubled at first by this. This soon passed and she fell into her duties. I guess it's a proclivity for men like us to have second thoughts around the time of our crowning. Much like how maidens have second thoughts after they put their wedding dress on, handed the flowers, and take a last look in the mirror before they make their way to the alter on a wedding day."

"Hmm, yes that sounds like the scenario I'm feeling right now."

"It'll all work out in the end. Just continue what you are doing and Providence will guide you through the rest."

"Why do women act like that, Geoff?"

"Well, the way I perceive it, even when women are young, they dream of nothing but being a princess or queen and would give anything to be pampered and treated like one. When they do finally receive the title, it is a dream come true for them and they simply become bloody shell shocked with awe at the endless possibilities of being royalty."

They came upon a hilly, grassy clearing where sheep grazed about a hundred yards in the distance. The whole area was shrouded by fog.

He turned to Charles. "This is one my favorite spots. Its one of the most peaceful places that I know of."

Charles listened as the breeze swayed through the grass. A brook softly ran through the hills, making the faintest trickling of water. The fog was now lifting and he could see the grandeur of the countryside. Geoffrey hopped off of his horse and led it to the stream while the foxhounds trailed behind him. As the horse drank, he reached down and patted and stroked its mane. Charles brought his horse over for a drink as well.

"How has your family been faring since I've last seen them? Your son George must be at least twelve now.

The King sighed and looked at Charles. "George . . . well, of course you know he has bone marrow cancer. They say his odds are not too splendid at the moment. My little son has had this damn disease for about two years. But he is bloody resilient and I believe he'll make it to be king someday after I've passed on." Suddenly, the men were interrupted by a loud hum in the sky.

They both looked up to see squadrons of the Royal Air Corps making their way to the Morcaster Instillation.

Charles looked at him. "Geoff. What do you think the outcome of this assault will be? I mean do we really have a chance at winning this world war. Let's face it; we're on the brink with the entire Western Hemisphere. We are already at war with Russia and Germany. We've tried negotiating with Alejandro and Alexandra. None of these four countries' has a leader who possesses the comprehension of compromise. It's like negotiating with barbarians and Neanderthals."

"We will if we strategize right. The day we give up is the day hell freezes. With any luck, in a few months High Chancellor Warrenhari Zeithen will be as dead as Julius Caesar. If we want India to join us in our cause, which they've already shown interest in, it will be up to Pacifica to coax them. India is a little cheeky when it comes to coordinating with their old administrative empire."

"I find that odd considering India won independence from you over a thousand years ago."

"I guess old habits die hard, my friend."

He looked over to the hill of sheep upon hearing them stir up from something. The dogs began to whimper and bark.

"I think we've found our first fox!" Geoffrey quickly mounted his black horse and crossed the stream with the dogs. Charles followed behind. The sheep began to cry louder and in between the running sheep was a lone, red fox.

"When I let loose the dogs, you take off after that bloody fox. When you come close enough, you make the call on when to shoot it. Just don't shoot the hounds in the process. It would be a shame considering they are some of the finest foxhounds. I'd say get about four meters away then let him have it!" said the King with such conviction that he nearly lost his balance.

"Careful there, Beowulf. I don't want you to break an arm before the first shot is even fired," said Charles.

King Geoffrey laughed, and then let out two whistles. The foxhounds took off towards the frightened sheep. Charles took his rod and whacked it against the side of the horse. It took off and leaped across the stream. He was surprised at the speed at which it traveled. The fox began making its way over the hill.

Behind him, the king was shouting as he tried to keep up with Charles. "Don't lose him, he's going to try to head for the woods."

The fox did just that, and the hounds were unable to change their direction. Charles pulled his revolver out of the holster in the saddle. He cocked it back and aimed for a spot to the right of where the fox was heading. He fired two shots and the fox quickly changed direction.

"Bloody hell! I never thought of doing that before, Charley!" yelled the monarch admiringly. The fox shifted so quick that Charles' horse almost gave out from underneath him. The hounds kept the little red animal on a narrow path through a rocky pass. The horse was constantly slipping on rocks and Charles was almost certain that it was eventually going to fall down along with him.

The hounds were slowing down now and began to trail behind between Charles and Geoffrey. The grass was getting taller between the rocky pass and soon all he could make out was a trail of beaten down grass where the fox had run.

Charles called out, "How big is the pass, Hamlet?"

"It should end about in about a hundred meters or so. Just brace yourself for the drop off,"

"Drop off?"

"Its about a meter and a half. The horse should make it."

Charles could see the opening to the pass, as it got wider. The horse was now catching up to the speeding fox. Its panting was visible in the cool air. He withdrew his revolver again from the leather holster hoping the fox would stop and make a stand against him and the hounds.

The pass abruptly ended within twenty feet. He gave the horse a nudge with his boots to prep it for the jump. The horse leaped over the ledge. Charles felt exhilarated for a moment when he was in the air but quickly felt fear when the horse landed wrong on the ground and sent him skidding through the grass. He lay there for a moment assessing if he had injured himself.

Other than his white pants being stained green, he felt but a little winded. King Geoffrey and the foxhounds stopped at the ledge. Charles' horse got back up on its feet and trotted back to him. He was certain the fox was gone.

"Sorry Geoff but it looks like he got away from us."

The King talked in a hushed tone. "Charley, keep quiet. Chap, that damn thing is going to bite your bloody face off if you don't shoot it soon."

Charles, still sitting on the ground, stared for a moment reorienting himself of the situation. His adrenaline made his heart beat faster as he made out the low growling from behind him. Without turning around and looking at the animal, he reached up towards the horse and slowly removed the revolver.

The hounds started barking. Charles turned around and saw the fox was low on its front two legs, signaling aggression. As it lunged at him, Charles cocked the revolver and fired two shots.

The animal fell to the ground after a moment, and then remained still. Charles prodded it a little to see if it was limp and dead.

"Good show, Charley! Jolly good show! That is one of nicest pelts I've seen in months!" Charles picked up the fox and began to walk it over to the King. "A present for my host and friend."

King Geoffrey put up his hand. "No, no. It is *your* earned trophy, Caesar." Charles smiled at his friend and hung the fox over the horse's back.

Geoffrey turned to him. "'Tis a gift from England to you."

<u>CANTO V</u>

Premier Vladimir Boris Nevski sat brooding at a desk in the Kremlin, listening to one of his closest friends in the Party 'politely suggesting' a loosening of regulations on the food industry.

"Maybe if we could just install a new beef plant in Moskva, we would be able to bring in a little more revenue, Premier. If we could put the food and medicine industry under the Perestroika Clause, we would be able to pay off the military debt a little faster. That way we could focus on steel and iron production that has been falling short of its quota the past two years."

"That is called Capitalism, comrade," said Nevski, rubbing his head. "Do you want to spend Patriot Day at the rally or in the Lubyanka?"

"Oh no no no, Premier. I was just trying to think of ways to put the current debt behind us as soon as possible."

"Well call me again when you have another idea." He hung up.

Aleksandr Kavojovanovski, the Vice Premier, began to walk into his office. "Tell the servant I need another drink."

Aleksandr stuck his head out the door. "The Premier would like another drink."

He came in and sat down in front of Nevski and lit a cheap cigar. "The Pacific Empire recently sent a convoy to London. KGB believes the Emperor is meeting with the King for the outlines of a military ordinance of some kind." The Vice Premier always liked to believe that he was the first to deliver all the latest information to the Soviet Premier.

"Yes, I'm aware. The Head KGB lieutenants in St. Petersburg contacted me about an hour ago. Thank you though."

"Oh, well, all right then."

"I'm also aware that the Brotherhood of Nikolai has mobilizing in the Kamchatka, the Crimea and Alaska."

"Better in North America than in Russia."

"No comrade, not better. If they base themselves in Alaska, they will constantly be jumping across the Bering Strait and we will be doing the same and frankly, comrade, they are already starting to do that. The line in the sand is slowly sweeping west towards us. Village by village, base by base, farm by farm. Our only instillation in Alaska was lost to them four months ago and now Vladivostok and Magadan are next on the list! How can we win a war with Prussia if we can't even keep our own country in line?"

"But Premier, it's our land! We can go where ever we please."

"Swelling troops into Alaska to quell those pigs would stir up the Americans more than we want. We are already a spitting distance away from clashing with them. We have enough on our plates as it is. Pissing off the Americans would be like stepping in a big, smelly pile of govno."

"I suppose you are right."

The servant came in and poured Nevski another shot of vodka. "You can leave the bottle here."

"Yes, comrade."

"Thank you, Dasha."She turned and left his office. He turned to Aleksandr,"She is one of my favorites out of the whole Kremlin staff."

He smirked, "Agreed. Mine too."

Outside, blizzard winds pounded on the office windows and shook the whole Kremlin. "I think this one of the harshest winters we have had in eight years. The snow is five feet deep in only forty-eight hours! Do you think America gets this much bad weather?" They both laughed.

"No, undoubtedly not, my friend. A peasant could easily stand out in their weather for days without so much as being in discomfort."

Nevski looked at his watch. "Well, comrade, I have to attend a meeting in the war room in two minutes."

"I have to attend too. I will follow you down there."

The two got up and left the office. As they were leaving, Nevski turned to the servant. "Dasha, I would like another bottle in my office by the time I'm back."

"Yes, Premier."

In the Soviet war room, General Yuri Radakov pointed at a holo in the center. "Six more ICBMs will be ready for the hell march on Patriot Day. Unfortunately, we received word that the 89th and 203rd garrisons station in Siberia will not be marching in the Patriot Day hell march because about forty-eight hours ago, we confirmed that over half of them had frozen to death in their barracks during the power outage that night."

"Why was nothing sent to them? This seems like a very preventable crisis," interjected Nevski.

"Emergency fuel had not arrived in time. The nearest town was out of fuel because no Lunex supply had arrived due to the winter shortage. It was negative sixty-nine degrees Fahrenheit."

Nevski's face tightened. "How many men?"

"Over four hundred."

Nevski slammed his fists down onto the table. "Damn!" He looked down the long rectangular table at all the attendees. "Do you realize that we are at war? Do you realize that the Prussians are bearing down on the Soviet people every moment we waste? Stupid mistakes like this are the reason we cannot push them back to Germany! Morons like you are the reason communism looks like a failed utopia to the rest of the world. You incapable pigs are supposed to be making the country run smoothly but instead it is going to hell! If Premier Litovka were still alive, you all would have been executed by now! He is the reason central Asia is now *Soviet* central Asia. He is the reason the Arctic Circle bears the red flag and he is the reason that Bolshevikvia was a juggernaut for over sixty years!"

The attendees in the war room avoided his gaze. He could feel the stress and fear radiating off of them. He fed off of anxiety like that.

"We are on the brink of civil war, comrades. The Brotherhood is gathering. Over two-thirds of our forces are pitted on the western front. The East is defenseless. It is open and ripe for the Brotherhood's plucking, like a herd of sheep without a shepherd. Our forces are preoccupied. The Soviet bear is in the West and these dogs that hide in Alaska are poised to pounce. If they catch wind that over four hundred troops in Siberia froze to death, it will only sweeten the deal for them."

Yuri stood. "Fellow comrade, what do you want us to do then? We are short on troops. They have all taken arms against the western front."

Vlad stared at him for a moment, and then opened his mouth. "Any man of seventeen years to thirty-five years east of the Ural Mountains will be drafted, college bound or not. The two-year service will be extended to however long they are needed. Farmers and production workers with seniority will be exempt. Everyone else goes. Now Yuri."

"Yes, Premier." General Radakov saluted him and left the room.

The holo projector in the center of the table flashed on. Nevski seated himself as an image of the King of Arabia came into view. "Good afternoon, neighboring Soviets. Have you considered our oil proposition we prepared last week? We *do* have much oil to spare."

"Da, and what was the price per barrel again?" asked Nevski, looking at a folder containing the oil exchange information.

"Seven hundred rubles per barrel, Premier."

The Premier tossed the folder over his shoulder. "Seven hundred rubles? Is that so?" Nevski looked the King in the eyes over the holo. "Well here is what I have to say about your oil. Fuck your oil, King! Here in Bolshevikvia, we can give our children fifteen rubles and they will roll a barrel of Lunex home to us. Do you know why? Because for starters, our Communist system is perfect and thusly the cost of it is cheap as govno. Second, we have means of getting to the moon. On the other hand you have no way of getting your sandy, brown asses up there and we like it and plan to keep it that way and buying oil off you would only promote your efforts. Fuck you and your bourgeois system."

He leaned back in his chair. "And I know something else about you Arabian. Yes I have been informed that you have been supplying Pacifica with top-of-the-line, new prototype tanks. Are you trying to play double agent or something, King? You are lucky that I don't sweep down from Georgia right now and finish you Muslims off!"

"The U.N. would never allow you!"

"Oh wouldn't they? What can they do? Look at the map, King. Egypt, Israel and Bolshevikvia are the M.E.U.'s only neighbors. I *am* the U.N. now! The only reason I don't order every garrison in Central Asia to rain down on the M.E.U. is because I get much more enjoyment watching you all dry up in your little sand huts under world economic sanctions, and watch you beg for a trade deal from me to bring in any sort of revenue. I get much more pleasure out of this than I would watching the Bolshevik armies storm your few remaining cities. Although you have no idea how many times I've been tempted to do that to Mecca—."

The King terminated the frequency.

Nevski looked at everyone else. "Govno, I was just getting warmed up." They all nervously laughed. He put on a stern face and threw another folder onto the table. "Now then, as for production quotas for the past two months . . . they were disgraceful!"

Yuri Radakov walked toward the entrance to the Kremlin. A decorated man stood at the door waiting for him. It was Sergeant Valentino Konstantin a long time friend of Yuri he met in the academy. They began to walk out of the lobby together.

"What did the Premier say, comrade?"

"He pretty much gave the biggest draft order ever made, my friend."

"What are the details?"

He sighed "Every man between seventeen and thirty-five. No farmers and factory workers with long time seniority. Everyone else is pretty much enlisted already."

"Oh God . . . my son—"

"Mine too."

"How are you going to execute this?"

"I'm going to have to head back to headquarters and send out the message. It will have to be executed in every town across eastern Russia."

"My God, can he do that?"

"He can do anything he wants to. He's the Premier. I just wish my son, Vasily, wouldn't have to be dragged into this, along with the rest of Mother Russia's sons. I'm going to try to see if I can get him sent into the air force to be a mechanic there. That's what he is now in Kazakhstan. He will be relatively safe. I'll see if I can do the same for Ivan."

"Thank you, comrade." As they rounded the corner, two Soviet mega planes flew overhead. Their loud roar was deafening. The mega planes were nothing like Pacifica's space planes. These were simply like a *P38 Lightning* that were used during World War Two that were enlarged twenty times its size. The mega planes were significantly slower than the space planes and could not achieve a high enough altitude to be considered a spacecraft. They were green and black with a giant red star on both sides and were as big as a city block. "They must be heading back to Gagarin Air Base." Radakov noticed that the tail of the one was charred and mangled. The plane also had a tilt to it, as if it couldn't fly straight because of the damage. Konstantin sighed. He whispered to Radakov,"Sometimes, comrade, I wonder if we are on the wrong side."

Yuri was startled by his comment. "Quiet! There are cameras around everywhere comrade," he whispered. "The KGB will hear you!"

"But we are whispering, Yuri. The wind is howling today."

"KGB can still hear you. Just stop. Please, you'll get us both in some deep govno. More eyes are on officers like us than the average person."

"Fine. Be like that, like a frightened little dog."

"Spare me, comrade. Are you off duty?" asked Yuri.

"Yes. I am taking a taxi back to my apartment. They gave me leave for the day but I must be back at headquarters tomorrow morning at six for the Patriot Day Hell March. You?"

"No, that is out of the question. I have to be back at headquarters soon with the orders and then I leave for Finland for our assault on Denmark in three days."

"Hmm. Well, good luck." A taxi stopped at a red light. Valentino tapped on the roof of it. The driver looked at him then quickly had the door lifted."

"Where to, Sir?"

"Second Harbor Avenue."

"Yes sir."

He put the window down and stuck his head out. "Don't worry too much about Denmark. Just take it easy tomorrow. You'll need your strength."

"I'll make sure Ivan isn't thrown into the infantries."

"I know you will. I trust you." He saluted Radakov and the taxi drove away. Yuri continued down the sidewalk. He started to replay what Valentino had said over and over in his mind. "Sometimes, comrade, I wonder if we are on the wrong side." He did not know what life would be like without communism. He had never experienced anything different. He had read about what it would be like but he couldn't tell if was true or not and he dare not tell anyone that he had read blacklisted books. It wasn't the first time that books were rewritten to favor the current state of Russia. A black vehicle pulled up to Yuri.

"Grand General Radakov."

"Yes?"

"Is there a reason why you are walking alone in the city during this storm?"

"I just accompanied Sergeant Konstantin to a taxi. Is there a reason why you are taking that tone of voice with me, comrade?"

"Sorry General, but as you can imagine, we don't like high ranking officers walking back to headquarters by themselves. This is a dangerous city and the KGB bureau would prefer that we take you back ourselves, now if you please—"

Radakov reluctantly opened the back door and got in. He closed the door. "Thank you, General. We will be back at headquarters in a few minutes."

Radakov nodded.

Valentino Konstantin opened the door to his apartment and flicked on the lights. It was the first time he had been home in months, but the stuffy smell made it feel more like years. He took off his coat and hung it on a rack along with his hat. He walked to the cupboard and pulled out a bottle of vodka and a cheap cigar out of a box. He walked into his living room and turned on the TV and changed the channel to prime time news. A perky woman with blonde hair appeared on the screen.

"In later news, the Pacifican Armada his increased its naval ships in the Atlantic. More were spotted by spy satellites moving around Patagonia and into the Mid Atlantic for reasons unknown."

Konstantin laughed at the TV. "Ha! I might be able to think of a few!"

"The Emperor of the Pacific Empire was spotted by KGB spies in London today meeting with King Geoffrey of Britain. He arrived today in the Charles II Military Instillation along with three Pacifican space planes. Speculators might infer that these two nations might be coordinating an attack. On whom they will assault is unknown."

"A man was arrested today for selling black market products at an unlicensed stand outside of—" He poured out some vodka and then grabbed a match and lit the tip of his cigar, then puffed on it.

Outside he could here some type of commotion from the street. Men were yelling and giving orders. He could hear some of his neighbors talking to whoever was out there. He disregarded it, then laid long ways on his couch and puffed again on his cigar. As he began to set it down in an ashtray, the tobacco fell out of it and onto his neck and burned it a little. "Govno!" He quickly wiped it off and tossed the cigar into a nearby ashtray. The noise grew louder outside, but he was still too careless to get up and look out the window. He took his glass and drank the vodka down, then stared up at the ceiling fan, daydreaming and zoning in and out about how much he hated his job. How much he hated the war and the way Bolshevikvia was run. He hated the Premier and the KGB. He hated all the surveillance in the streets and anywhere he went. He hated the way his life was going in general and began to imagine himself living in countries that he thought were happier places to live in. He imagined living in a harmonious place such as the Orient. Then in a bucolic setting in England, somewhere in the grassy hills where he could have tea with friends and go fox hunting now and then. He even imagined himself living in Pacifica, only having a duty to God and the Emperor. Two things that his own country would perpetually deny him. He felt a longing that he could not describe. Such little structure in such nations yet perfectly harmonious in all ways. They did not need the government to live happy and fulfilling lives. It seemed like there was a real reason that they all believed in a Deity of some sort and it was evident in all their success and happiness.

The noise outside was now disturbingly close to his front door. Just as he lifted his head up to get a better look, men in black bashed in his front door and rushed over to him. He sat up and then felt one of the men beat him over the head with a wooden nightstick. He could feel the blood running down his forehead. They threw him to the floor and put cuffs on his hands. He looked up at the man standing in front of him.

"Sergeant Valentino Konstantin, you have been charged treason and have been condemned as an enemy of the State. Do you have anything to say, pig?" asked the stark man.

Valentino put his head down. "Take this filthy dog away." The men in black grabbed his arms and dragged him out the front door . . .

Moscow, Patriot Day; 9:30 a.m.

Yuri Radakov stood in front of dozens of garrisons waiting in uniform to march down Red Square as soon as the ballistics and ICBM missiles were done being paraded through. On his right and his left, commanders and officers were whispering amongst themselves. Sergeant Konstantin was supposed to be there with his battalion. He turned to a captain. "Where is Konstantin? He was supposed to be here an hour ago. I don't see him or his battalion."

"General, I'm sorry, you didn't hear?"

"Hear what, comrade?"

"He's been executed."

"*What?*"

"He was charged with treason. The KGB heard him on the streets yesterday from the cameras that he was questioning his loyalty to Bolshevikvia. They arrested him at his apartment and sent him to the Moscow Detention Center, where they sentenced him, I guess. But what do you expect for saying traitorous thoughts out loud in front of a street camera. A traitor deserves a traitors death, don't you think?"

"Uh—yes— . . . of course."

The captain raised her eyebrow with a suspicious look. He avoided her gaze. It was a well-known fact that he and the Sergeant were long time friends. They were seen everywhere together. His body started to shake and shiver and his bowls started to feel queasy. Thoughts of paranoia started to fill his head.

The drums of the band in front of them began to beat. He was already in motion and moving into Red Square with everyone else and didn't even realize it. His vision began to blur and sway as his mind filled with dread and fear that he would be next. The Square was filled with red banners that had portraits of famous leaders such as Stalin, Khrushchev, Medvedev, Kavoijonov, Itazhenska, Urusov, Litovka and Nevski. Red and yellow confetti fell from the sky as they made their way into the center. To their left were hundreds of spectators with a platform at the top of the bleachers, where Nevski, Kavojovanovski, and many other head Party members stood gazing at the armies below.

The captain looked over at him. "Are you ready?" he said to her. She nodded. They got to a certain point in the square and then in unison yelled, "*Garrison salute!*" They all turned to the platform towards the Premier and saluted him and the others. Yuri's dread soon turned to rage as he glared at the Premier when they marched by. He saw nothing but red around the Premier and it was not from the banners either. "*I can't stay here any longer*," he thought to himself. He put on a fake smile for the Premier. Nevski nodded to him with a sign of approval. He clenched his hand into fist on the opposite side of his body. He recalled what Nevski had warned everyone about in the War Room. "*The Brotherhood is gathering . . .* !" he squeezed his teeth tight together as his blood began to boil with anger towards everyone on the platform above . . .

CANTO VI

Charles splendored from the cool, salty spray of the sea as the *HMS KRAKEN* split the ocean surges in two. He was in awe of the Kraken because he had never actually been on it or its sister before. He felt no swaying, no rumbling, and no shakiness. The waves bowed before the vessel as it led the way to Iberia, with the rest of the Imperial fleet trailing behind.

Grand Admiral Mozzollio approached him on the deck "Is there any way I can get armor as nice as that?" he said, examining the Emperor's new brass core body armor. It was a custom that when the emperors of Pacifica went into battle they wore a white outfit with a brass armor that covered only torso and core but not the arms and legs. They also always wore a roman style Galea with red feathers and would have the royal sword sheathed at their sides though they were not obliged to use it and then lastly their weapon or weapons of choice.

Charles laughed. "The sad fact is, it won't look this good when we are through with this ambush. In fact I probably will get rid of it depending on how much I am shot at. But, if you *really* want it . . ." Mozzollio smiled. He had to squint painfully to look at it. The sun was shining so brightly in the blue sky that it reflected off of it and into his eyes. He turned away. "How far away are we from Portug—"

Someone came in over the Kraken's intercom. *"Attention all personnel, we are twenty-five kilometers from away from Iberia. All personnel are to begin dispatching and unloading procedures now."*

"I guess we have an answer, your majesty."

"I suppose we do."

He looked up at the sky for a few minutes and saw gulls gliding gracefully in the wind above the deck. He felt an odd but comforting presence of some kind but could not describe it. It was soothing, almost relaxing feeling.

Gregorian monk chants played over the intercom of the entire ship of not just the Kraken but all vessels. The music was standard procedure. It was a technique thought up by Charles' own father to calm the troops and crew before battle. There were also priests walking throughout all the ships talking to the troops and comforting them. It was a way for them to ease their nerves and make peace with the Almighty before battle, that way they could initiate in combat without holding anything back whether it be their conscience or their fear of dying, they would be at peace yet operating to their fullest potential. It proved to be quite effective too.

"It truly is a beautiful day today," said Charles. "A shame that it's ending won't be as beautiful as it's morning."

"It is a necessary evil, sir."

"Yes, I'm afraid so." He looked backed up at the gulls, crowing in the wind. "What is our outcome percentage, Grand Admiral?"

"Our numbers right now are sitting at eighty-nine percent, you highness."

"Not bad, I like the sound of eighty-nine. We need to save our strength for the Pyrenees. It will only get tougher when we travel inland."

"Oh yes I don't doubt that at all. I will make sure the Kraken makes our landing as quick and painless as possible."

"Yes, Vinney, I have much faith in you. You're a good Admiral, I trust you, my friend."

He felt honored. "Thank you, your eminence." He bowed low.

"Attention all personnel, we are fifteen kilometers away from Iberia. Last minute procedures should be carried out immediately. All personnel are to report to turret stations and shoreline dispatch off-load areas now."

A man ran out to the deck where the Emperor and Grand Admiral Mozzollio were. He bowed to Charles and saluted Mozzollio. "Grand Admiral! We have info from Imperial Intelligence that the Germans are aware of our offense. General Di'Orlo wants to know the plan of action and of any altercations you wish to infer."

The Grand Admiral looked at him. "The space planes should be in position for when we land on the shore, not to mention there are three space planes docked on the Kraken's landing pad. If our ground troops get into a sticky situation, we will test out a little gift from our Muslim friends."

"Yes, sir." He saluted again, and then walked back inside.

"A gift from the Muslims? I was not aware," said Charles.

"The King of Arabia gave us a state-of-the-art, new super tank they had been working on for decades. It was a gift to the Pacifican Holy Army for your coronation. They named it 'The Hammer of Allah.'"

"What is special about it?"

"The armor is almost impenetrable, it's two stories tall, has four sets of treads instead of the normal two so it can travel over any terrain, multiple cannons, can squish a building flatter than a piece of matzo bread, and can bust its way through a town to make paths for our armies."

The Emperor smiled, "Well, I accept then."

"Attention all personnel, we are three kilometers from Iberia. All orders will be given from your appointed officers in any later time."

Charles stood on the command deck inside the Kraken, looking down on multiple levels of the Herculean ship below. Mozzollio approached him. "Your majesty, everything is set for the assault. We will be there momentarily."

"Very good, Admiral. Bring King Geoffrey up on the holo."

The King showed up on a holo. "What can I do for you, Charley?"

"Are you all set for the assault, Geoff?"

"Bloody well, my friend. Everyone aboard has the spirit of Beowulf in 'um," said the King.

Charles smiled. "Good to hear. Now then just a reminder, the Kraken will spend about five to ten minutes, charring the German forces on the shore in an inferno of rockets. The space planes will land and the rest of the navy will dock along with the British. After we land on shore, we will make headway to Madrid and Barcelona. From there we will meet up with the Spanish army and begin to repel the Germans across the Pyrenees."

"Indeed. I will see you on the shore, then?"

"Yes, you will. Good luck." Charles turned off the holo.

"Two kilometers from dispatch," said a voice over the intercom. Charles turned to the Grand Admiral.

"I want to say a little something to everyone before we depart. Put me on all of our vessels." Mozzollio handed him a small square device. He put it up to his mouth. "Attention my fellow Pacifican brothers. This is your Emperor, Charles Augustus. In a few moments, you will be storming the shores of the Kingdom of Spain, to confront the German barbarians. We are here . . . to take the first steps towards bringing peace and human rights and freedom back into the world. As of late, the world has been falling into a disarray of oppression and dictatorship and genocide. We will not stand, as an Empire, to let the globe stray from what it was intended to do. You could say . . . we are taking the first steps towards world peace. But this won't happen without war. Zeithen believes that the Muslims and the Asians should be exterminated like vermin from the face of the earth. We will bring the hammer of judgment and justice down upon Zeithen and the German barbarians!—" The ship began to roar with cheering

"One kilometer from dispatch."

"—The Lord watches over all of us like a good shepherd. With Michael on side, we will send them back to the Stone Age! I pray that the Archangel himself will follow each of us into battle today. Just remember, my brothers, when your legs feel the burn of running, when you are disoriented from battle, when the earth harshly meets your feet with every step, when the mid day sun aches you vision, your Emperor is there, experiencing it all with you." The ships cheering got louder. "We are all in this together as one. Not just countrymen but as the human race. Do it for justice. Do it for humanity. Do it for your late emperor who was shot down and out of the sky by the barbarians! I too will do my part, just as much as you will, in the epic to come. God be with us."

The kraken slowed to an abrupt stop and the ship quieted down. Charles knew what was to come. Mozzollio was talking behind him, coordinating men and women at control panels and computers and was talking on multiple holos to various ships through out British and Pacifican naval fleets.

"Can I get a conformation now?" he asked.

A woman turned in a chair to him. "We're clear to go, Grand Admiral."

Vinney turned to the Emperor. "This is it."

"Its time."

Vinney looked back at them. "*Fire!*"

A hellfire of rockets and missiles boomed out of every cannon of the two fleets, leaving them in a black cloud. Mozzollio squeezed the chair in front of him. "Wait for visual conformation. The cloud lifted and no sooner than it did, the bucolic shoreline turned into an orange inferno. On various screens throughout the command deck, Charles could see Panzers and Stingers moving over the dunes preparing to fire.

"Sir, we missed multiple stations behind the hills," said a man.

Charles was appalled. "How is that possible?"

"It does not surprise me, your majesty. Most of their barracks and warehouses are underground," said Mozzollio. He looked at the command deck. "Resume the bombardment."

The shore exploded again, throwing and tossing the retaliates hundreds of feet away. Again, nothing was visible.

"We're picking up enemy aircrafts coming out of the base."

"Ready the turrets by the time they are in view."

"Yes, Grand Admiral."

General Di'Orlo appeared on a holo in the center of the command deck. "Grand Admiral Mozzollio, I believe we are in position to dispatch the troops. The King is getting very eager to land over on this side of the fleet. Can you give a target time?"

Mozzollio laughed. "We're taking care of a few bombers coming out of the base, then we will dispatch."

"Stupendous." The general's holo blipped out.

Charles was flabbergasted behind him. "This seems too easy . . ."

"Why yes, your majesty, it is. That was the whole objective. They were not prepared for us therefore they are now running around like chickens with their heads chopped off," said Vinney, as the last of the bombers were shot out of the sky.

"Yes, I suppose your right."

Outside, one of the German bombers crash landed on the deck of the Kraken and exploded into an orange ball of fire, but apparently caused no damage at all to the Kraken's deck. "We'll get the janitorial staff on that after this," said Mozzollio. The command deck staff laughed. A woman looked at him.

"Sir, we aren't picking up anything immediate on our radars."

"I think we should tell General Di'Orlo its time to dispatch."

"Yes, sir."

Mozzollio looked at the Emperor. "Your majesty, are you decent?"

Charles put on his helmet. "Tell the King I'm ready . . ."

Tens of thousands of men dotted the shore from below the hill that the Charles and King Geoffrey stood on.

"Would you look at that. Absolutely marvelous. Only twenty-three men have gone off to Paradise. The rest are leaving for Seville."

"Good, laddie. Today was a victorious day for both of us."

"Indeed. But we cannot stay here. We have to keep moving."

General Di'Orlo approached the two of them. "Your majesties, we are assembling over the hill over there near what is left of the base. We want to be on the road to Barcelona in fifteen-behind you!"

A German soldier sprung out from the bushes with a dagger. Charles quickly took his sword out of his sheath and stabbed the man through belly and withdrew it. The man quickly crippled to the ground and then laid still and quiet.

"Bloody good, Charley. For a moment there, I thought you'd be joining your father there."

Imperial soldiers ran around a bend to the Emperor. "You majesty," one of them said in a mechanized voice through the speaker in his helmet," this is a dangerous area. If you please, you need to be on the space plane now. The more time we spend here, the more opposition we will have when we get to the Pyrenees."

"They're right, your highness," said General Di'Orlo. "We must leave now, we're using up precious time." He turned to the squad. "Escort us to the space planes."

"Yes, sir."

As they left for the vessels, men with flame-throwing devices entered the little German underground base. Di'Orlo saw Charles looking at them. "They'll finish the demons off." Charles nodded his head with approval.

"How far away is Seville?"

"About half an hour by space plane. Resistance will minimal there as well. The Prussians have not been here for more than a month so naturally the Spanish Army has been very quick to respond."

"That's to be expected. And Barcelona?"

"Five days, most likely. And that's if we play our jigotties right."

Four days later . . .

"We have conformation that all seven legions have been spaced equally along the Pyrenees Mountain range, camped at various passes and roadways. Nothing is getting in or out of Spain without us knowing. The eighth legion or as we have nicknamed the German Extermination legion will being double backing through every major city in Spain to make sure this country is no longer a safe haven for them." He pointed at the map on the holo inside the tent. "After we resupply and bring in reinforcements our next major objective will be Paris, while British troops head east, but for now, lets just get settled hear. We'll pick off anyone who tries to cross the range."

"Zeithen is too smart though," said General Ravenwood, head commander of the British military, "I'll tell what that cunning fox will do. He'll use our own strategy against us. He'll swell troops to the south of France. He'll make sure nothing from Europe gets into Spain. He'll starve the country of every resource possible. We're here to help Iberia, not make things worse. The more we hang around here, the more information Zeithen will have on us. *We need to strike now!* He's in the south of France with Gottschalk and Gustav!"

General Di'Orlo was taken back. "That's ludicrous! We don't have what it takes right now! We'd need the eighth legion to scramble back up here and abandon the extermination. Nor do we have the resources! Are we forgetting why we are here? The Germans were making a beeline for Italy! This was meant to be a distraction so that we could buy the Italians time reinforce their army, so that they could defend for themselves, so that one of the last free countries in Europe would not have to salute the flag of Germany."

"*But we could end this right now!* You damn bloody fool! He's no more than a hundred miles away! This could be over *NOW!*" Ravenwood yelled back at Di'Orlo.

"Do you *really* think that High Chancellor Warrenhari Zeithen is just sitting on the other side of the Pyrenees by his lonesome, twiddling his thumbs and playing 'patty cake' with Gottschalk? Over three quarters of the S.S. branch is on the other side. That's hundreds of thousands of elite, blonde haired, little demons all dressed in black that wouldn't bat one of their blue little eyes for a moment at blowing up each and every one of us. We can't afford it. The only thing that is holding them back is that the passes are too narrow for them to over run us. Thank God we made it here in time otherwise they'd already be pouring through the passes."

Ravenwood looked at King Geoffrey. "I'm sorry laddie, but he's right as rain on this one."

He looked back at Di'Orlo. "Damn you." He stormed out of the tent. Di'Orlo straightened himself out and pulled on the bottom of his uniform to get out the creases but said nothing for fear that the Emperor would be displeased. Pacificans were always taught to have a strong backbone when it came to taunting and to never retaliate a verbal aggressor. It was just a trait that was common among all citizens of the Empire that stemmed from the Church's teachings of loving your enemies.

The cold, snowy wind howled against sides of the large tent. Charles turned away from Di'Orlo to look at the dozens of people stationed at computers and satellite equipment operating and talking to multiple people, from the Grand Admiral on the Kraken to units and squadrons still Seville and Madrid to coordinators on multiple space planes. They all looked exhausted, as if they had been doing it for days on end. He thought of something to say to them, to lift their motivation a little. "Phenomenal job to you all. Pacifica is very much obliged to you for your skilled services."

"Thank you, your majesty." They all brightened up a bit and continued to work with a little more zeal than they had prior.

Charles smiled as he pulled his coat a little tighter to himself, trying to keep warm in the frigid air. He had no idea it was going to be this cold. He walked over to General Di'Orlo. "I believe I am going to retire for tonight. It's three in the morning. Have someone clean my sword and the sheath. I pulled it out of the sheath this morning and realized it still had the blood of those German devils all over it. Good night."

"I will. Good night, my friend." They gave each other a bear hug and then walked away. Charles opened the flaps to the tent. Wind and snow rushed in and blow the fur hood off of his head. He heard a strange low sound from outside. A type of dull humming, coming from the north in the sky. He pondered for a moment.

He looked over his shoulder. "General, do you hear someth—"

"*Bombers!*" screamed a woman managing satellite images at a computer. "Hundreds of them!"

King Geoffrey sprang over to her before General Di'Orlo could even turn around. "Good God, it's a bloody retaliation assault!"

The General grabbed a mike from a box on a post. "Red alert! Red alert! All personnel report to turret and gun stations now! Incoming German bombers from the north. This is not a drill. Everyone is to don NiteVis' now. Base camp lights will be cut off in thirty-seconds!"

Lights were always turned off during attacks to lessen the chance of precision bombing of camps. Everyone put on night vision goggles to eliminate the need for lights. In the meantime, troops would be shooting enemy aircrafts out of the sky.

"Charles, put these on!" The Emperor put them on over his head and turned them on. He again opened the flaps and looked to where the loud humming was coming from. In the green sky, through his goggles, swarms of black aircrafts made their way past the mountain peaks. Turrets and gun cannons ignited with bright flashes as rockets and missiles poured out of the hundreds of anti aircraft barrels like water. The hellfire soon pounded the bombers in fiery explosions in the sky. Some landed on the slopes, others kept their dooming flight path towards the Pacifican encampment.

The Emperor walked to a stack of cased weapons. He opened one. Inside was a StingerSmart Launcher. Di'Orlo pulled it out of its foamy casing. "Do you know how to use this?" he yelled above the loud explosions in the sky.

"Not at all."

"Load the package in the back. Look through the scope, lock on the target and fire. That's all there is."

The General took off to the front of the camp to coordinate the turrets. Charles noticed a clump of two dozen soldiers or so that were lined up in position behind some crates that were lined up in a row for firing protection. He ran up to them and positioned himself in the center of the row. They all looked at him, astonished and honored to see their Emperor fighting along their side, as he had promised aboard the Kraken. The sight motivated them and he knew it. He looked through the scope to pick out a bomber.

As he looked closely he noticed that one had made it past the turret defenses and was no longer able to be fired upon by them. General Di'Orlo turned around at him. *"Emperor Charles! LOOK OUT!"*

He aimed the scope at the bomber and pressed the lock button. It beeped in acknowledgement. He squeezed the trigger and three missiles fired out of the launcher. The force of the launch almost knocked him off his feet.

The bomber ignited into an orange inferno as it soared past he and the soldiers only a few feet above their heads, so close he could make out the swastika on the side against the orange fiery glow, and then loudly exploded upon impact of a Lunex fuel tanker.

The soldiers triumphantly jumped up and cheered, throwing their fists in the air as well as the men operating the turrets at the front of the encampment who had witnessed what had happened. "All hail the Emperor!" They all yelled unanimously. Charles smiled in acknowledgement. He heard a man from behind him cry out. "They're turning around!" The cheering got louder. Charles heaved a sigh of relief. He grinned at the sight of the remaining bombers turning around and crossing back over the peaks of the Pyrenees Mountains.

"Today is going to be a good day," he thought to himself.

CANTO VII

A rather malevolent looking man stood watching the last of his defeated bombers return from the other side of the Pyrenees, with his fists clenched in his crossed arms. His coat blew around in the wind as the snow was driven into his face. It made no difference to him. He rarely felt any emotion at all, but vengeful or victorious. He was about as stone cold as the ground he stood on. The man is Germany's High Chancellor, Warrenhari Zeithen and right now he was about as enraged as his comrades had ever seen him. He had already broken a soldiers nose when he had reported to Zeithen that the bombers had failed to break Pacifican defenses. The man who was coordinating the attack was already lying on the frosty ground with a bullet in his head a few meters away.

Oberst Gottschalk, one of the many military advisors to Zeithen approached him cautiously. "Chancellor, shall I fetch a coroner to take the captain away? He will stink up the camp soon if he lays over there for too much longer."

"Let the ravens eat him."

"Yes, sir. As you wish." The amazing aspect about Zeithen when compared to his S.S. officers was that even his head S.S. Lieutenants couldn't stomach some of the orders that he could do all by himself. Gottschalk hated when rare defeats like this one occurred during the Campaigns. Zeithen was so used to getting his own way in war that when he did lose a battle, it was like being punched square in the face while he was asleep. Gottschalk tried to cheer him up a bit. "They won't stand a chance this winter. I'd wager that they don't even have the supplies. They'll be scrambling back to their little tropical continent when the storm in the North hits."

Zeithen slammed his fists down on the table in front of him, smashing a light and the computer on it.

"Edvard! If we can't even break this little blockade, how are we supposed to "relieve" the King of Spain if we aren't even present *in* Spain? We were supposed to be in Morocco two weeks ago! The Muslims still remain! We were to begin our foothold on our war on Islam in Morocco. Rid Africa, the cradle of humanity, of the unwanted Arabs that snaked their way across thousands of years ago, and push east. Subsequently wiping out the Muslims. A Teutonic, Christian rule that reigns from Iberia to the Ganges River. But, we are two weeks behind."

"Sir, there are many German soldiers in Spain. We air dropped them in weeks ago."

"They're dead. Or at least they're going to be. Not only is Spain in the last stages of a German purge but apparently Britain and the Empire of the Pacific is there to assist."

His wife, Hermia approached him from behind. She was usually one of the few people that could settle him down but her chances were not good this morning.

"Warrenhari, I'm getting cold. When can we cross the range into warmer weather? I want to be in Madrid. Why is it taking so long to get to Madrid?"

Without looking behind him, he flung out his arm and struck his wife in the face with his fore arm. She fell onto the snow-dusted grass with a sore cheek. Hermia got up with a disgusted look on her face and walked away.

Hermia never really got any respect from her husband and her husband never received any from her either. They both deserved the misery sown between the two of them. Zeithen was a cold man and husband and Hermia was a self centered and cunning woman. When she gave birth to her first child she felt that the constant elements of a baby, such as crying and feeding and cuddling, were too much of a burden because it cut into the time she spent on social networks and her interest in the fashion world. During a blizzard one night, at their estate in Nuremburg, she left the baby girl out by the mailbox to freeze.

Zeithen looked back at the cowering men standing erect before him. He stared them down for many moments. Even in the freezing temperatures, they sweated profusely.

"If you keep sweating like that you'll be picking beads of ice off your face when you return to your barracks."

They embarrassingly turned to leave.

He called out to one of the men, "Kommandant, you and I are not done here. You have already failed the Fatherland once, and I pray that you will not do so again. Be in the battle room in ten minutes with an idea that will save your ass from 'special' camps where failures like you are condemned."

"Ja mein Führer, it will be done."

The High Chancellor turned around and walked away, soon veiled by the blowing snow, into the darkness of the night.

In the battle room, Zeithen stood in front of a table with his hands sprawled out in front of him, glaring at the frightened air commander. "Kommandant, I trust that you have come up with a little something better than what we attempted four hours ago."

"Yes, High Chancellor. The main attack should not come front but from the sides. It would be to our benefit if we combined a Pincer and Blitzkrieg attack. What we need to do is take a garrison out of the Elite Stosstrupp through the Central Pass to make them think we will swell everyone into it. The reality is we will split our air forces in two by about fifty miles where they will attack Pacifica and the British from behind while they are preoccupied with the Elite Stosstrupp. The moment they take their eyes off of the lone garrison is when we swell our ground infantries through the Central Pass! This is a great ambush tactic that Hannibal used to beat the Roman Army at the Battle of Cannae. It worked quite well."

The High Chancellor stared coldly at him. No emotion. No feeling. Just a look in his eye that made him look like a phantom. His fingers retracted into a fist. The veins in his forehead stuck out and pulsated. His jaws were clenched together, causing the muscles in his neck to flex. He let out a sigh but it sounded more like an irritated snarl. He soon relaxed and his fist flattened out on the table.

"If you fail again, do not even bother showing your pug face around any Germans because you will be shot on sight. There is not a demon in hell that will be a greater terror to you than I."

"Without question, High Chancellor."

"Come. It is time the Romans are beaten again."

The airfield at the base of the mountains where the German bombers were grounded was covered in snow from the winds of the approaching storm. As the first light of day turned the sky from black to gray, mechanics scrambled to repair the damaged bombers and brush the snow off the remaining ones. The Elite Stoss Truppen or Shock Troops were arranged in neat uniform ranks waiting for orders from the Führer.

"The time has come," said Zeithen, "to finish God's work. The Moslems will continue the devil's work until we cross these mountains. Kommandant, you may now scramble the troopers."

The commander put a little silver device to his mouth. "All troops scramble positions. Bomber liftoff is in two minutes. Hiel Zeithen."

"*Hiel Zeithen!*" Hundreds of Shock Troopers took off in perfect ranks towards the Central Pass in uniform step, leaving a trail of footprints in the snow, along with jeep like vehicles and other transports. The commander turned to make his way towards the command room. Zeithen grabbed his forearm.

"Where do you think you are going, Kommandant?"

"I must keep in contact with the bombers when they reach the enemy encampment, Chancellor."

"No, I don't think that will be necessary today. We have plenty of coordinators that will do a sufficient job. Go with the ground troops. Get your weapon of choice from the armory cache and get in a Jeepen with the captain."

The commander froze and was only able to stammer an, "Of course."

He turned and walked away. This was his punishment for defeat and he knew it. Going with the ground troops in the German military for high-ranking officers always meant certain death. He prepared for the worst.

On the other side of the Pyrenees, King Geoffrey sipped on a cup of tea, talking to his head commander. "The bloody defense system the Pacificans brought with them worked like a charm. Put up one hell of a fight last night, those Prussians did."

"That they did, your majesty. I have a hunch that we have not seen last of them. The Pacificans are at the northern end of camp and thus they saw the most action."

"Yes, well it is nine A.M., they should have had their tea and biscuits by now. I'll be damned if they aren't ready for more encounters with the demons," said the King.

"To tell you the truth, I doubt they got too much more sleep after last night. Most of them were putting out fires. Others were surveying the wreckage and seeing if there were any survivors from the crashes. Two pilots were found at the base of one of the mounts. General Di'Orlo had them placed in detention containment cells aboard one of their space planes. No doubt they will be "coaxed" into talking."

"As well they should."

A soldier approached the King and bowed to him. "General Ravenwood, three Spanish garrisons have arrived under the order of Commander Segovia." A decorated man appeared from around a vehicle and bowed to King Geoffrey.

"Buenos Dias, your majesty. My name is Commander Eduardo Segovia. My men and I are honored to fight along your side for the survival of Spain. My King sends his regards to you and the Emperor and is very much obliged."

General Di'Orlo interjected just as sirens rang out again through the entire encampment, "Well it would appear that you came at the precise time. Commander, we have word that German Shock Troopers are funneling through the Central Pass."

"We will halt them! Just make room for the garrisons to run through the camp."

General Di'Orlo nodded and Segovia picked up a primitive looking brass pendant that hung from his neck and blew on it.

"What is that, a whistle?"

"Yes is it. It is my pride and joy."

"That must be a thousand years old."

"One thousand two hundred to be precise, amigo."

Di'Orlo looked at some of the mechanics that were scrambling about. "Get those Lunex tankers out of the way! We need to make room for the Spaniards."

"Yes, General."

From behind Di'Orlo, men in olive green uniforms hurried forwards towards the front of the encampment. "*To the Pass!*" yelled the Commander in Spanish at the soldiers rushing by. "*Tri formation!*"

Di'Orlo put a comm-pod to his mouth. "Turret defenses 4-A through 9-A, why are you not firing? They are in your range!"

His comm-pod crackled then a voice replied. "We can't, General. The snow is blowing around too thickly in the wind. We can't see them and we probably won't be able to pretty much until they're within spitting distances!"

"Tell the captain up there to have you and the rest of them take defensive positions. Three Spanish garrisons will be on the offensive. They should be passing you momentarily. Assist them whenever you are able to."

"They're passing us now, General. We're taking defensive positions."

"Maintain."

"Yes, sir."

He put the pod back in his coat pocket and put up his fur hood as he watched the tail end of the garrisons hurry by.

Charles approached King Geoffrey, Di'Orlo and Ravenwood.

"What's the situation, gentlemen?" he asked.

"The German barbarians are trying to squeeze through the pass."

"The stinger launchers are over there if you need another one," commented Di'Orlo. Charles smiled at him. Di'Orlo's comm-pod beeped and he picked it up again. "What is it, Captain?"

"Opposition seems to be minimal, sir. I don't understand. Why would the Germans send in a garrison and not more? I thought there would be more. And why waste a garrison of Shock Troopers? I can't— . . . wait . . . Sir we have captured one of the head German commanders! He's extremely wounded though."

"Get him into a medical pod and have him sent back to one of the space planes for treatment."

"Yes, sir. But as far as the garrison, I just don't understand."

"Yeah, that's pretty weird. Hmmm, just see if Segovia can sur—." A familiar, low humming sound came from the sky, but he could not pinpoint where it was coming from. A British soldier ran out from behind a tent.

"*BOMBERS*!" he screamed to any one who was around.

"Again?" Charles exclaimed.

"Your majesties, you must get to somewhere safe. Visibility from the snow is too low to dodge anything the bombers drop on us. We have to get to the command room to see wha—."Di'Orlo's comm-pod came to life again.

The Captain in the north of the camp started hollering. "General! The Shock Troopers were a distraction! They are pulling a Pincer on us! What should we do?"

"Maintain the defense! For all we know these bombers might be a distraction too and the rest of the Germans will swell the moment we take our eyes off the pass! Maintain the blockade!"

"Yes, sir!"

In the command room, Di'Orlo and Charles watched as the bombers neared the encampment on a computer screen of one of the coordinators. The woman looked at them. "This snow is making things so damn worse. Our defenses can't see a hundred feet in the air. They are gonna roast us into sirloin steaks."

"What about our auto targeting defenses? Why haven't they been activated?"

"They won't be as accurate and besides, they're only capable of taking out one plane at a time given the space."

"They're packed like sardines," said Charles.

"Its because of the snow. It's so they won't criss cross and crash into each other," she said.

"We're sitting ducks." Charles started pacing with anticipation. The first of the assaults from the bombers made a loud boom as they hit the far west and east side of the encampment. He threw his head back in disdain as he listened to panicking soldiers scrambling outside. "Those space planes are our only way out of here. If they hit them, we are going to be stranded here in Iberia for a long time.

Di'Orlo slammed his fist down on the table. His mind spun wild with a feeling of dread and helplessness, like sheep waiting to be slaughtered. His mind raced, trying desperately to think of something. He thought of what Charles had said about the bombers being packed tightly together. His eyes brightened with an epiphany "If they're so tight together, and if the auto defenses are turned on, a missile sent to the center of the group would cause multiple bombers to explode." The people sitting at the computers and equipment systems perked up. "Think about it. They're *so* close together that the explosion would affect multiple enemy aircrafts! It wouldn't matter if it missed one because it would just hit the next one behind it!"

The woman's head spun around to him. "Of course!"

"Turn them on, now!"

A man two seats down spoke up. "Initiating auto turrets defenses now." Charles watched one of the screens as multiple turrets sprang to life and began a hellfire retaliation of missiles and rockets into the snow filled air. Everyone in the command room turned to the holo of the encampment in the center of the room that pictured every thing that was going on. Charles got close to it and watch the little blips of light that were missiles travel towards groups of little aircrafts.

"Come on," he whispered. "Come on!" A little flash of light occurred and seven little Prussian bombers on the hologram burst into tiny infernos, hurling towards the earth.

Everyone in the command room sprang up and cheered. Another group on the west side flashed and eight more went down.

Charles patted Di'Orlo on the back. "This snow was a gift from God," said Di'Orlo. "Had it been clear weather, we would have never pegged off this many barbarians."

"I know, General. We have much to be thankful for."

Di'Orlo smiled and looked at the members of the command room. "Maintain the bombardment. Make sure we have plenty of mechanics servicing and restocking the auto defenses."

"Yes, General."

High Chancellor Warrenhari Zeithen stammered with utter rage as he could hear the bombers explode and crash on the other side of the Pyrenees. He clenched his fists so tightly that they were beginning to bleed. One of his teeth was already chipped from squeezing his jaws to tightly.

"Gustav. What has become of our beloved Kommondant?"

"He was severely wounded eight minutes ago. We haven't heard anything from him or the Captain."

"Has he been brought back yet?"

"No, the Pacificans dragged what was left of him away."

"Good. Maybe they can use him for fertilizer. That's all he was ever worth to us."

"Yes, indeed," said Gustav.

The High Chancellor of Prussia turned his piercing bloodshot eyes at Gustav, almost as a precautionary warning to him to not fail in his duties, then walked off into the blustering snow.

CANTO VIII

Five weeks later . . .

Charles and Di'Orlo descended the ramp of the *HMS Triumphant* with Octavia, towards an enormous cheering crowd, accompanied by four E.I.T's. Lights flashed from reporters and camera crews alike as they shouted questions that were barely audible over the 'all hailing' of the crowds. The Emperor smiled as the tropical heat rushed over him. The cold altitude of the Pyrenees had made everyone on the blockade miss the tropical continent. He watched the reporters follow him along the barricade with an array of questions.

"Your majesty, can you recount what the repeated attempts by the Germans to break through the blockade of the Pyrenees was like?"

"When will the Italians be mobilizing across the Alps?"

"Is it true that you yourself blew up a bomber that flew overhead of the camp?"

Charles couldn't help but smile at that one. "Well, something along those lines." Di'Orlo laughed and looked at the reporters as he led the Emperor down the purple carpet. "He will be giving a royal address to Pacifica, tomorrow evening. That is all you need to know right now." He looked at Charles. "By the way we may have another front opened up to us.

He stopped and looked at Di'Orlo with disdain. "What do you mean another front?"

"This is actually positive news, your Majesty. We received word on the way home that the Brotherhood of Nikolai II has just attained a vital figure in the Russian resistance. They want to meet with us at the Beilski Instillation in Anchorage."

"Who is it?"

"We don't know. They wouldn't say, but whoever it is, it must be important."

"Tell the Brotherhood that we will arrive when they are ready," said Charles as they walked alongside the cheering crowds.

Charles looked at Octavia. She had the same look in her eyes that he had seen on their coronation day; that look of subdued ecstasy. He thought about the advice that Geoffrey had given him, about waiting the phase out. He sighed and looked at the crowded people that were waving and jumping up and down to get his attention. They held big velvet banners that had IFPP and the Imperial crown and trident blazoned on them. As Octavia waved to the last of the crowd before she was escorted into limousine, Di'Orlo extended his hand to help her in with the Emperor.

When the Emperor entered through the entrance to Edward Palace with the Empress, Giuseppe and Cipriana raced towards him. He caught them both and carried them as he walked to one of his studies. "Father we're so happy you're home. I thought the Prussians had got you."

"Ha! Well, no, but I got one of them," Charles chuckled.

"That's what they are saying on the tele and the holos. Mother was starting to worry a lot," said Cipriana.

"Was she now?" Octavia smiled and rolled her eyes. She looked at the Emperor.

"Can you blame me? I couldn't even talk to you."

"No, my sweet Empress I cannot. But if I were to send out a signal, we would have given away our position. How has the Empire been while I was away? I hope the children didn't behave too badly."

"They couldn't hear enough about you while you were gone. It was very brave of you, Charles, to go off to war with your soldiers in a foreign land and I think the people were very proud of it."

"I just wish my Father was here to see us."

"He did. He probably had a better view than you did. And I'm sure he was with you every step of the way."

Charles smiled. "Thank you, Octavia."

"Children, do you mind if your father and I talk for a moment?"

They both left the room. "How are the children?" asked Charles.

"They are doing well. They both are advancing in their education. Cipriana is one of the brightest young girls in her mathematics classes."

"That's fantastic. I'm glad to hear that." Charles looked at a huge bouquet of flowers that sat on his desk. "Who are these from?"

"Prime Minister Yosef Steinam of Israel sent those to you two days ago for your arrival home. It is something of a thank you gift on behalf of Israel and the rest of the M.E.U. He also sent some bottles of wine, some roast lambs, and a few Arabian laser-guided ballistics missiles to thank you and Pacifica for the assault on Germany in Iberia."

"Roast lamb. That sounds exquisite. We should have it for dinner. I'll make sure Di'Orlo and Mozzollio come. They'll be pleased to hear about the missiles. Arab weaponry is a point of interest for both of them."

She smiled and laid herself down on a nearby couch. "I missed you," she said as she ran her fingers over the blue velvet cushions.

"I missed you too. The Pyrenees was a cold and lonely place," he said as he lay down beside the Empress.

"Why did the King of Spain only send three legions to assist you?"

"That's all they had, Octavia. The rest were on a man hunt for the remaining Germans that were secretly air dropped in."

"I think they could've spared a few more," she said, crossing her arms. "I think they were sitting back and letting us fight it for them. That's what I believe. They should be showing more respect to an empire that is there on a charitable whim. They should be forfeiting Portugal to us for all our hard work. We're the reason the Germans are starting to be repelled back to the north."

Charles sat up. He was startled and confused that Octavia was talking like this. Especially since it was he who was present in Iberia and not her. "Octavia, how can you say that? We are Pacificans, not conquistadors."

"Charles, I'm surprised that you don't agree with me. You yourself were over there. You saw how we were bombarded and mowed down. It's only fitting."

"Octavia, that's what makes us different from Germany! We're not land lusting heathens."

She got up. "I just—, never mind." She walked out.

Charles sighed and sat himself at his desk. He swung his chair around to look out over the balcony.

He heard the holo projector on his desk behind him blip on.

"Your majesty," said a course Russian voice. He sprung around and almost jumped out of his chair. The holo showed the head Soviet General, Yuri Radakov.

"How did you—"

"Forgive me for hacking into your holo but I felt it would be much safer if this was a one on one with no prying eyes."

"What threats does Nevski have to bring to Pacifica today?"

"I no longer am an instrument of Bolshevikvia. I am the "vital figure" that the Brotherhood has acquired. You could say there has been a change of favor. As you know, with Iberia, Italy, the Middle East and Bolshevikvia bearing down upon Germany, the troops will soon be retreating back to Germany. When this happens, Bolshevikvia will move west. Much like it did in the twentieth century. The Brotherhood feels that in order to keep history from repeating itself, the moment that the Prussians retreat is the moment the Brotherhood should strike at Bolshevikvia."

"That is a very tactically smart move of the Brotherhood."

"Those who do not learn history are doomed to repeat it."

"That is exactly what I teach my son."

"You and I are not so different. I have many secrets of Bolshevikvia that will be employed soon. That is why we need to meet as soon as possible. You too might benefit. How soon can you get on a space plane to Beilski Instillation?"

"Don't you think it would be wise if we waited for Prussia and Bolshevikvia to battle it out and see who the victor is? That way they would be too weakened?"

"We intend to but the Brotherhood needs a plan ready for when the time is right. Is forty-eight hours sufficient, your Highness?"

"For I, yes, but you really should contact Imperial Intelligence. They need to make preparations for this."

"Yes, we are already one step ahead of you. They should know by now. Whatever you do, don't bring any extra escorts. This is meant to be a low profile meeting. We don't want to attract any more attention than we already have. Too much commotion will stir the Soviets like a hive of hornets. We aren't ready for that kind of action yet, your Majesty."

"You have to understand though that Pacifica is already enthralled with Germany. Lets not jump into one more problem than we need to."

"Germany is not finished but it is retreating in defeat at an incredible rate. You just happened to enter at the tail end of this war. All we have to do is continue the offense."

"I don't think this will be the last of them, though," said the Emperor.

"That may be, but why do today what you can put off till tomorrow. If Germany shrinks down far enough, we won't need to worry about them. Someday after Bolshevikvia has forfeited to the Brotherhood, we can finish off Germany."

"Yes, I agree."

"Alaska is becoming a stronghold for the Brotherhood of Nikolai II. More men are secretly crossing the Straits to join the resistance. The Heir of course will greatly reward the Pacific Empire if you join our cause."

"The Heir? I'm sorry, I'm not sure if I know who you are referring to."

"The Heir? Why, he is heir to the throne of Holy Mother Russia. The Romanov's family tree had many sprouts that grew off of it. Though the royal family was executed, they still had many distant relatives that they were probably not even aware of. They hid in Alaska for over hundreds years, for fear of assassination. But now that Bolshevikvia's citizens are becoming more and more displeased with their situation, the resistance was started by none other than the long time in hiding heir. He changed the name from the Resistance to the Brotherhood of Nikolai II after his late, royal relative. He is the head of the Brotherhood and will soon be the new Emperor of Holy Mother Russia. Unfortunately, he cannot do it without Pacifica and other nation's help and support."

"I'm sure England would be more than willing. There's a large concentration of forces currently in Australia in New South Wales and Queensland."

"They are next on my contact list. I will leave you now, your majesty. I hope to see you in two days."

"I just have one more question to ask of you. What made you turn on the Soviets? You were one of Nevski's greatest and closest commanders. He let you make every decision on the battlefield without ever questioning you. I don't understand."

"They executed my best friend. He was saying traitorous thoughts out loud on the streets and KGB cameras caught him. They broke into his apartment that night, beat him half to death, deemed him an enemy of the State, and sentenced him to death by the 'smoosher.'"

"Dear God, what is the 'smoosher'?"

"A concrete slab that is slowly lowered over you mechanically until you are as flat as an American pancake."

Charles crossed himself. "Thank you for the invitation. Tell the Heir we will be in Anchorage in two days."

"The Heir greatly and humbly thanks you for your graces." Yuri bowed to Charles. The holo bleeped off, leaving the room in utter silence.

The wine in Di'Orlo's cup glistened from the light of the chandelier above. The room was filled with the smell of roast lamb and the last of the sun was setting over the palms.

"Imperial Intelligence got a direct holo from the Heir an hour ago," said Mozzollio, wiping his mouth with his napkin.

"Radakov and I were having a chat too. He seems quite intent on us meeting the Brotherhood in Alaska as soon as we can."

"That doesn't surprise me in the least. I mean they have been waiting for an opportunity like this for hundreds of years. The sooner they get to their goal, the better," said Di'Orlo. "This lamb tastes great. So tender . . ." He put another fork full in his mouth.

"I think that our aid with the Brotherhood will be very rewarding for Pacifica. Maybe even a little chunk of land as a thank you present," said Mozzollio. "Resistances in the past have always been grateful to us for our assistance."

Charles took another bite of the lamb, then a spoonful of the Israeli Prime Minister's specialty garlic hummus. "We have our work cut out for ourselves."

"What do you think the Brotherhood has that makes them so sure of themselves?" asked Octavia.

"Besides Yuri? They have an entire instillation at their disposal. A surplus of food, water, medicine, war vehicles, an airfield. The works. They have the makings of a great resistance force," said Di'Orlo.

"Well, that's good news for us, indeed."

"I agree completely, your majesty," he said to the Empress.

Octavia sipped her wine. "Yes, I agree with the Grand Admiral. Resistances have always been good to us. I'm sure they'll grace us with the Kamchatka or something," she lightly added.

"Our continent is big enough. Much of it still isn't even developed yet, let alone explored," said the Emperor. "Lets just harvest what we have first and then we will make the call."

They all nodded.

Octavia's eyes wandered towards the window, where the clouds glinted with a soft hugh of pink from the sunset in the red sky. The cathedral bells rang out from their towers in New Rome amidst the commotion of the city. She ran her fingers over the gold handle of the ceremonial dagger in her overcoat garment, listening to the head military commanders of the Empire converse with Charles.

CANTO IX

Thirty-six hours later, Charles could hardly believe that he was already back on the space plane, bound for another cold corner of the world. The Bering Sea roared below the *HMS Emperor Tiberius II*. He felt the snowy wind jostle and jolt the aircraft as it soared over the merciless ocean. Ice began to build up on the mega glass dome that bulged out from under the belly of the vessel, making it harder to see down below. He shivered. It was hard to keep such an open aired section of the space plane heated. His bulky, white, fur hooded coat could not seem to sustain a comfortable temperature.

As he pulled it tighter around himself, he looked over the rail and down below to the ferocious sea. It pounded against the frozen, jagged rocks that jutted out from the stormy surges. Whales occasionally breached the waves for air, waited to make sure their calves surfaced behind them, and then plunged back down to the dark blue abyss.

General Di'Orlo approached from behind him along with another General, Catharine Olympos. They both stood at the rail along side of him, looking down below at the ocean. "We'll be landing outside the Beilski Instillation momentarily. Oh, excuse me, this is General Catharine Olympos. She is our newest addition to the Holy Army."

She stood erect before the Emperor. "A sacred honor to meet you, your Highness. I was at Imperial headquarters when we received the holo from the Heir. He seemed very eager to make an alliance between Imperial and Russian forces. He also appeared to be somewhat mysterious and what I mean is that he was cautious to not say too much or give us too much information. We could barely make out his face on the holo, he kept in the shadows."

"Makes sense. He has no allies yet. What do we know about him, General?"

"Imperial Intelligence has it that he is about fifty years of age. He wears a black, wool coat, tall black ushanka and has a short, trimmed beard."

"A stereotypical Russian."

"Yes Admiral. He is the very distant relative of the Russian Emperor, Nikolai Romanov II. His ancestral relative during that time was Nikolai's father's cousin, Vasily Romanov, who lived in the Kamchatka Peninsula. He had helped in the financial aid of the Trans Siberian Railroad and decided to live at the end of it after the conquest of the East. When the Soviet Revolution took place and the Bolsheviks took the empire, he hid in the Kamchatka as a peasant under the surname of Leonov. The Leonovs hid there for over a thousand years until recently when the current heir decided to come forward when the resistance was born. Regrettably, that is all we know."

"Did he say anything about what he proposes to do?"

"No, he did not, other than that he urgently needed to meet with you to discuss possible water treaties and a coalition between Pacifica and Russia against the Soviets."

"General, I know that you are new to the ranks but a word of advice. Before you have your royal Emperor embark on journeys to foreign lands, make sure we have all the information and objectives of the diplomat before hand. That way we can at least make sure the trip was not fruitless and a waste of Lunex."

"Yes, your Majesty. Please, forgive me."

He sighed, "I do. I just need a little more thought process out of my head military commanders when situations like this present themselves. I hope I'm not scaring you too much. You are new to the ranks and I don't want to discourage you."

"I build off of constructive criticism, your Majesty."

"Splendid. That will be all, Catharine."

In Pacifica, no one was addressed by his or her last name but rather by his or her Christian birth name. It was the same principle as a boss telling his employee to call him by his first name except backwards. If a Pacifican was acquainted enough with someone, he or she would ask them to call him or her by their last name but even this was rare.

She gave him a blinding smile and turned around to walk away. His eyes followed her. The general's outfit complimented her form. Charles quickly caught himself and turned away.

He turned his gaze to Di'Orlo. "How much farther do we have to go, General?" He rubbed his hands together to heat them up.

"We should be there in six minutes. The coastline should be visible soon in the—" The space plane accelerated forward, causing the two of them to practically lose their balance. "Admiral Kalani, what was the meaning of that," asked the General.

"Sir, we came across a school of Soviet nuclear submarines traveling eastward below us. We didn't want to take any chances. In a few moments we will be out of firing range."

"Thank you, Admiral."

"Lets just hope that was our only close call."

Hovering over the Alaskan landscape, the crew of the *HMS Emperor Tiberius II* diligently searched for a place to land near the Beilski Instillation. One of the personnel on the command deck pointed to his screen at a spot on a map. "There. This is flat enough for us."

Di'Orlo looked at him. "Any obstructions?"

"Other than the trees, no."

"Descend."

As the vessel's intercom began to announce to its crew, Charles watched the tree line crawl closer and closer to him.

Space planes landed more like bulldozers than delicate aircrafts. When a space plane lands, it smashes anything underneath it, whether it is trees in a forest or buildings in a city. All that ever mattered was that the vessel be balanced after it landed. If it wasn't, there was a risk of it rolling onto its side. It would be like a city block of metal rolling over and crushing everything beneath it. This type of accident only occurred once before, in Italy, when Charles' grandfather met with King Alfonso. It was a spectacular sight for the locals to witness. It fell over onto its side, and then slid like a humungous sled down the ocean cliff. There was never an attempt at restoration and the ship still sits in a hulking, metal ruin on the rocky shoreline to this day.

Landing in an uncleared area always made for a bumpy landing. Charles grabbed hold of a rail on the command deck and braced himself. The light was soon smothered out by the forest tree line and the ship shook ferociously as the trees around it all snapped simultaneously and so loudly that the Emperor could neither hear anything or anyone for several moments.

Finally, the movement stopped and the vessel stabilized itself with its landing gear. The Emperor watched the horizon readjust from the command deck.

From below, ramps and mammoth sized ports opened and various ground vehicles drove out, escorting a MammothV-7 transport, along with various falcon interceptors that shrilled out of the launch bay.

General Di'Orlo, still leaning over the rail next to him, looked at Charles. "Well, should we precede?"

"Very well, General. The sooner we get to the instillation, the sooner we can make our way home. I'm freezing, even with this coat on."

"I hate to be the bearer of bad news, your Eminence, but we may be here a while. We don't want to fight someone else's revolution and I feel that we should make it prevalent to the Heir," said General Olympos from behind him. The Emperor looked back at her.

"We don't want to stay here too long though, General. Do not think that the Soviets are oblivious to our visit to one of their lost republikas. This needs to be swift and declarative. If we over stay our welcome in this tundra, it will give the Soviets even more of a reason to send waves of troops to Alaska. Not only will they storm the Brotherhood but they will also wipe out everyone on this little diplomatic journey."

"Of course, your Highness. My mistake."

The Emperor smiled at her. He admired her zeal and conviction. It was inspiring to see young, new commanders put their minds and hearts into their occupational tasks of the empire.1

"Come, let's board the transport. Our Russian friends are waiting."

The transport made its way through the forest at about thirty miles per hour while assault vehicles filled with E.I.T.'s protected it on all sides. From inside, Charles jolted around in his seat with every tree that the Mammoth transport knocked over to make way for the rest of the convoy.

"We're coming up on a clearing, your Majesty. We will be at Beilski in a few moments," said one of the drivers.

"Thank you, soldier."

Mozzollio leaned over to him. "The General will get out and have the Russians open the gates for us. We'll drive across the airfield to the instillation and you will be escorted out by the E.I.T.'s."

"Why would he have to get out? I mean that makes no sense; I thought we were living in the year 3012 not 2011 or something like that! How would they not know we are coming? Are they honestly that far back on the evolutionary scale? Are *we*?"

"No your graciousness, we have been in contact with them for the whole trip, the Russians are just squirrelly, that and they want to welcome him. You know how they are."

Charles shook his head and rolled his eyes back. From the front windshield of the mammoth sized transport, he could see Di'Orlo's jeep-like vehicle speed in front of them to the front of the convoy as they made their way across the frozen tundra.

"What an unforgiving land to live in," said the Grand Admiral.

Charles smirked. "The Russians are a very hardened people. They have endured more than just weather. They've become accustomed to it." He leaned back in his chair. "Besides, Russians are proud of their winters. The harsher they are, the more toughness is attributed to them. Kind of like how Pacificans are proud of their hurricanes, only with blizzards"

"I suppose your are right. But me personally, I like my estate on the western Kiakalani coast."

"Yes, I wouldn't ever dream of leaving New Rome either."

When the Pacifican continent rose out of the Pacific Ocean, it completely changed the jet streams, gulf streams and any other type of stream you could think of on that side of the planet. These altercations enabled South America to be the breeding grounds of ferocious hurricanes, much like how West Africa is ground zero for almost all of the hurricanes that ravage the American coasts. These hurricanes pound the Pacifican coasts mercilessly during the winter months every year. And every year the Pacificans resiliently recover within a few weeks.

The huge V7 began slowing to a stop. Charles looked from behind the drivers to look out the windshield. Outside, General Di'Orlo had already stepped out of the jeep-like assault vehicle and was conversing with some Russian guards on top of a large, metal-sheeted gate. They saluted him and beckoned to someone from behind. The gate began to slide open and the General opened his door and sat himself inside the vehicle.

"They're letting us in," said one of the transport's drivers to the other. "Ease it forward." The transport came to life again and followed the General inside with the convoy trailing behind it.

When they had driven across the landing field and found a suitable spot to stop, the side of the transport began to open. Charles rose out his seat, fixed his crown on his head, and approached the hatch. Four Elite Imperial Troopers positioned around him to escort him out, as was custom. When the hatch opened and the hydraulics stopped hissing, The Emperor descended out to be greeted by a group of five decorated, Russian commanders. Charles only recognized two of the five. On the inner right was the former Soviet General, Yuri Radakov. The man in the center, Charles guessed was the Heir, Viktor Romanov. He was a middle aged, charismatic looking man. His description perfectly matched what Catharine had given him on the space plane.

"Privet and Welcome to the new Russian Empire, Emperor Charles Augustus. I would like to say that you and the whole of the Pacifica are always welcome in my country."

"Thank you, Heir Romanov." Charles bowed to the Heir first, (since it was he who was the guest) then the Heir bowed to him and kissed the ring on Charles right hand (since the Heir was not yet crowned royalty. He was still below Charles; otherwise the ring kissing would not be necessary).

"Come my friends, let us get out of this blustery weather. We have much to discuss."

A door to a hanger bay opened and Charles, Di'Orlo and other Pacificans followed the Heir to the Russian throne inside.

The Beilski Military Instillation was poorly lit and littered with crates and containers full of supplies, weapons, and food for the exhausted resistance members. Along the walls, symbols, logos, and insignias of the former Soviet base were covered with crude graffiti at the hands of the Brotherhood inhabitants. The floors were covered with rubble and pieces of concrete and durawall. Charles had to be careful not to stumble on any of the broken weapons and rubble that were strewn about.

"You'll have to forgive Beilski's current appearance, you Majesty. Only recently did the Brotherhood extend its love to the instillation's former Soviet occupants and it still hasn't been completely cleaned up yet."

They continued through another hanger in the center of the base. It had a roof that at one time would open up for Soviet helicrafts to land. The roof was now rusted and partially open at the one end, letting a snowy draft in from the outside. Russian mototsykls were parked neatly in row after row and there were more piles of weapon crates here and there. There were a couple of barrels lit on fire with Brotherhood troops gathered around it to keep warm. The brothers saluted them as they walked by.

The hanger came to an end and they entered an executive wing that seemed to be untouched by conflict or the elements. They entered a pristine room that had holo maps along the walls. From the ceiling hung the flag of the Brotherhood of Nikolai II, which might someday be the flag of Russia. It was white and had the golden eagle of Russia on it in the center. In one foot, the eagle held the crown of emperors. In the other, it held the Orthodox cross. Positioned in the center of the room was a long, horizontal table in the center which also served as a large tactical computer screen to show army advancement details on a map. The heads of the Brotherhood all sat down on the one side of the table, the Pacificans, on the other.

Charles sat himself squarely in front of the Heir.

"My Pacifican friends," the Heir extended his arms in front of him, "the Brotherhood of Nikolai II is honored that you have considered helping Holy Mother Russia in this dark hour. We have requested your presence because, as you know, the Brotherhood would like you to consider a coalition with us against the Soviets. We are not asking you to fight our war for us and we don't want you to think for a moment that we want you finish off the 'Supreme Union' along our side. We simply need . . . a little starting nudge. A little more 'umph' in our fire power, when the time is right. We simply want to know if you will be there for us when that time comes. You see we too have the spirit of the Romans in us. After all when the Turks repelled the last of the Byzantincs from Constantinople, the refugees fled north and away from the Muslim threat. And when they went north, they eventually crossed into Russia, where they brought with them their customs, their language, their alphabet and their orthodox religion. That is why Russians sometimes consider themselves as the third Roman Empire although I'm sure Pacificans beg to differ." Charles smiled. "But regardless, the Brotherhood is preparing for a swift and calculated attack on the Soviets. Right now," the Heir pointed to a spot on a map on the long table," the Soviets are spilling into their newly acquired Manchurian region, and fortifying their borders with the Orient. They are also bordering up in their southern Mongolian front and the eastern Kazakh region border. The Soviets are also preoccupied with India. India has almost completely stolen Pakistan from the Soviets and now Bolshevikvia is about to retaliate against India."

Di'Orlo laughed. "They're just making friends everywhere," he said sarcastically.

The rebels laughed. The Heir began to speak again. "So as you can see, the Soviets have battlefronts on all sides *except* on their eastern coastline. That is where the Brotherhood comes in. We want to wait for the Soviets to swell their troops away from the Kamchatka, but we don't want to wait so long that they overwhelm Ito Yokomoto and the Asians. It would appear that the problem for the Orient is no longer at the hand of Zeithen but the Reds. We are looking at about a three day window coming up in two weeks from today."

Grand Admiral Mozzollio spoke up. "Where did you get all this information from in the first place?"

The Heir grinned and turned his head to Yuri. Yuri looked up from the table to the Pacificans. "You could say that I gave them a couple military fun facts."

They all laughed. The Heir pulled a bottle of vodka out from under the table. "Drink?"

Charles hesitated. Not sure whether to accept the friendly request or reject it for fear of poison, after all it was never wise gullibly drink something by yourself. But before he could come to a decision, the Heir had already downed a mouthful from of the bottle. "Ahhh. Made from the finest potatoes."

Charles shrugged and succumbed. "I'll give it a try." The Heir handed the bottle to the Emperor. Charles again hesitated. He wasn't used to the crudity of sharing and drinking out of the same bottle with other people. But he forced himself to momentarily let go of his royal mannerisms and take a swig. He accidentally took two swallows and it started to burn his mouth and throat. He put the bottle down and started to cough ferociously. The Russians on the opposite side began to chuckle. General Di'Orlo mustered up some courage and took a drink from the dark green bottle. He too started up in a coughing fit. By now everyone, Charles included, was laughing.

Di'Orlo put the cork back in the bottle and handed it back to the Heir. Viktor silently took another mouth full of the vodka and handed it to Yuri.

"So how many men are you looking for? What kind of fire power?" asked General Di'Orlo.

The Heir looked at Yuri for an answer. After a moment, calculating something in his head, Radakov began listing off what the Brotherhood needed, "One legion, two space planes—."

"*Two!*" interjected the Grand Admiral from the other end of the table.

Charles shot him a glance. Then calmly said, "We have one hundred and sixty-five in the Holy Orbital Force branch, Grand Admiral. Why don't we let our friend Yuri continue?"

Mozzollio leaned back in his chair. "Yes, your Majesty. I would just like to point out to the Brotherhood that Pacifican space planes cost over five hundred million natos, *each*." The Grand Admiral knew very well that the brothers (a title given to anyone who was a member of the Brotherhood of Nikolai II) did not have outstanding training. Though the Brotherhood had several training camps throughout Alaska, they were not 'grade A' camps in comparison to what the Soviets have. And with mediocre training given to the brothers, he was expecting that he will probably never see those two space planes again after the assault, nor the men on it, if it was the Russians piloting them.

He gestured for Yuri to continue. "—Eight BreacherX transports, and four Phoenix P-9 Dispatching Shuttle Landing Aircrafts; two for each space plane."

"*Even if* we give you these resources to work with for an assault, where would you even begin? I mean the Eastern shores are not huge but they are not small either. Do you even have a place of attack? Or what kind of naval support is in those waters?"

"Indeed we do. Ships are stationed south of Taiwan near the Philippines. A tropical typhoon that originated off of the province of Pseudo Africanus is hovering off the coast of China between Northern Taiwan and the southern tip of Japan in the East China Sea and is expected to do so for the next three weeks or so. This means that the ships are essentially are stuck there unless they are willing to make a complete circumnavigation of the Pacifican continent.

Those submarines, those poor excuses for orcas that were intersecting underneath you during your trip, are the only Soviet naval force that can safely travel."

"How did you know we intersected them?"

"We have many eyes watching the new Russia, Grand Admiral. Do you not think that we don't have Brothers in every branch of the Bolshevik military whispering back to us what our opposition is doing?"

"Please, continue."

"Like I said, the submarines are the only things fast enough that can make it safely to the Kamchatka."

Mozzollio looked at him as if he was crazy, "The Kamchatka? You want to land *there?*"

"Some of history's greatest empires were started on peninsulas and islands, Grand Admiral. Italy, Spain, Norway, England, Denmark, Greece, Turkey, Japan, India; would you not agree with this, Admiral Mozzollio?"

Mozzollio turned his gaze back at the table. "Well what do you have planned for the . . . Kamchatka peninsula, Heir Romanov?"

"Many Soviet troops left the base at the southernmost tip for Patriot Day for the three day long military march in Moscow. They have not yet returned. This means that the Kyenskovitch base in Petropavlovsk-Kamchatsky is largely empty. Intelligence has brought word that due to recent volcanic eruptions in the north of the Kamchatka and of the recent blizzard; power has been out for days in the city. The base is running on reserves and generators." He pulled up images on the table and around the room on the screens. "If we hit all three of these power stations and storm the remaining troops, the Kamchatka's only real source of national defense has been snuffed out, and the Peninsula will be under the royal rule of the Russian Empire."

"But they have multiple ways of knowing that we're coming. Its not going to be a secret once we take off for even two miles out into the ocean."

"I know. That is why we developed a plan for what to do as soon as we take off. We simply need to execute it quickly and flawlessly."

"And defense against the returning troops and the Manchurian swells? Volcanoes happen all the time. We know that more than anybody," said the Grand General. "The ash will eventually subside and the monorails and air traffic will start up again. As will the typhoon. What are you and the Russians going to do then?"

At every battlefront we create, roads and rails are destroyed. That is our policy and it always has been. As for the air traffic; it is winter. And winter in Russia is enough to keep a Supercarrier from taking off. That is another reason why South Kamchatka is so strategic and important to us."

"And the Soviet navy?"

"The people of the Kamchatka have been waiting for us for a long time. Russia . . . has been waiting for us for a long time. It is an unspoken truth that Intelligence can confirm just by the sharp increase in crime and defiance. The civilians are on our side. Also, I don't know how much attention you have yet paid to Kyenskovitch but its main function was to ward off attacks such as these. The whole perimeter is decorated with anti air and naval weaponry. With the typhoon and Kyenskovitch in the south, winter, volcanoes and destroyed lanes in the North, we have enough time and resources to train the civilians and ship over other Brothers from Alaska. The timing for all these events is perfect. You could say that it would appear that God is on our side."

Di'Orlo spoke up. "Let me ask you this, your highness Romanov, what's in it for Pacifica? What's the catch?"

The Heir looked back at him. "The catch, my friend?" He leaned back in his chair. "The 'catch' is that when the Brotherhood pushes the battlefront to the Urals, anything to the east of one hundred and twenty degrees longitude is yours. Which is right now currently one-fifth of Bolshevikvia's landmass, not to mention rich in deposits and agriculture." The Pacifican side of the table began stirring with whispers.

One of the Minor Parliament members leaned in towards the Emperor. "That would almost double the size of the Pacific Empire, your Eminence."

"A nice addition but it may too vast and relatively unprotected to our liking. Plus who's to say that the Brotherhood won't just stop a mile before the Urals?"

"True, but I have a feeling that the new emperor will eventually want Moscow and St. Petersburg, and well the rest of his country. Plus, if we do receive the land gift, we could appoint an Imperial viceroy to the region or even a provincial king. Subordinate to you of course."

"Provincial kings eventually let the title get to their heads though and they forget that they are not sovereign to the Emperor."

"Well then it would have to be someone from your bloodline, your brother perhaps? He is skilled in the Imperial political system and he has made it quite clear in the past that he would never comply to becoming emperor. The position might suit him better. And then from there, he could appoint the archdukes, grand dukes and counts."

In Pacifican Imperial hierarchy, The Emperor rules over the empire and if need be, he could appoint a subordinate king or viceroy (depending on the frame of ruling time) to a far away or vast province. Each province of the Empire was headed by an Archduke (or Governor, the title choice was left up to the appointed person; regardless the titles mean the same). Provinces are divided up into diocese much like how states are divided into districts in the Republic of North America (the U.S.) and are headed by Grand Dukes. Finally, diocese are broken down into parishes (much like counties in the R.N.A.) and are headed by a Counts or Countess.

"Hmm good point, Lord Guinero."

Charles nodded his head. The Heir looked back at the Emperor. "So, Emperor Charles Augustus, do I have your word?" He extended his arm to shake his hand. Charles looked at Di'Orlo for conformation. He nodded back at him. The Emperor looked at the Heir squarely in the eyes and grabbed his hand and shook it.

"Agreed, Romanov."

The Heir sat back in his seat and exhaled a sigh of relief. Charles stood up to leave along with the other Pacificans. They all shook hands with the persons across the table. "Thank you, my Pacifican friends for meeting with the Brotherhood today. You may have just as well saved Holy Mother Russia and we will never forget."

"We will be back in two weeks. Ready your Brothers," said Charles.

"Until we meet again, your Highness."

The four E.I.T.'s at the door escorted the Emperor out of the room, followed by the General, Grand Admiral and other commanders and members of the minor parliament. The Heir watched them exit.

"Two weeks."

The engines of the *HMS Emperor Tiberius II* roared to life as the Emperor stepped out of the elevator and onto the command deck. One of the men at a computer looked up at the Grand Admiral. "Are we clear?"

"All personnel are accounted for. You are go for launch."

"Understood. We are now island bound."

The space plane slowly rose up out of the dense forest. The blades under all four wings whirred as they spun faster and faster. The trees from underneath let gravity finish the job of falling. Soon the space plane turned a hundred and eighty degrees and began on its course south.

Charles took his usual position on the command deck at the railing where he could see everything that was going on. The General and the Grand Admiral approached him on both sides.

"I have a strange feeling," said Di'Orlo, "that the Soviets are going to focus all their attention on us after this little escapade in two weeks."

"What makes you say that?" asked the Emperor. "They still have even bigger problem, the Germans. We didn't even put a dent in their forces in Iberia. We simply created a foothold for ourselves and other European nations. And as long we keep the Pyrenees tight, nothing gets in."

"I don't know. That's just who they are, your Majesty."

General Olympos joined them at the railing, eager to hear what they had to say.

"Well, regardless, the reward for our help in this revolt is worth the chance," said the Mozzollio.

"A lot of land." Charles nodded. "A lot of land. I'm willing to take the chance if the rest of the empire is. Lets just take this one day at a time." They all shook their heads in agreement. The space plane started to shake again from the winds as they began to soar over the restless ocean, bound for their tropical continent. "I only fear that we will be involved in this longer than we want to be."

CANTO X

Outside of his executive chancellery office in Berlin, Germany's High Chancellor Warrenhari Zeithen watched the snow fall softly towards the ground, dusting all the trees and bushes along the way. It was calm. The city was exceptionally quiet this evening and he loved it. He could hear his thoughts with no other interruption than the ticking the crystal clock on his desk. He rubbed the top of the marble head bust of Handel, one of his favorite composers.

Zeithen shuffled through some of his papers on his desk to see which one he wanted to tackle first. He came across one that detailed his appearance at the Wittenberg Cathedral for Reformation Day in a few weeks in which he would be the guest speaker at the pulpit to give his annual theological sermons and give witness to newly anointed bishops of newly created synods in territory recently conquered by the forces of Germany. He looked at the paper underneath outlining the national art show coming up in a week in Paris.

Regardless of his image as the spawn of Hitler that the world had painted him out to be, Warrenhari was actually a very sophisticated and educated man with a deep appreciation for classical aesthetics and musical compositions. He seldom ever troubled his thoughts with war or politics anymore in his aging state. The High Chancellor was now sixty-eight years old and began to shift his focus from the map to the opera theater and the church. His church. The Lutheran Church. Zeithen was a devout Lutheran that stressed the revisiting of Germany to classical gothic cathedrals and churches that had everything that classical Prussia enjoyed when it went to services on Sunday. Lutheranism was the nation's religious identity. All other Protestant "imposters" were completely eradicated by the Reich earlier in his life. From Calvinists to Anabaptists, any false Protestant churches were an askew, twisted version of the faith and were completely expelled from the Reich. German citizens found guilty of religious treason had a year to convert or would face harsh "processing" (which most times meant execution). Zeithen theologically didn't have too much disdain about the Catholic Church existing in Germany, it's just that most of the High Chancellor's enemies where Catholic so it personally left a bad taste in his mouth. Consequently, Catholic Germans generally had harsher living parameters; such as higher taxes, fewer employment opportunities and restrictions on how much a parish could collect for almsgivings until the State would come and take the surplus that went over the quota. But since it was the Catholics who established the First Reich, they too were just as German as the Lutherans of the Second, Third and now the Fourth Reich. But since the creation of the Fourth, Zeithen discarded the ideology of congregationalism when he realized that Congregationalist churches throughout the Reich could be used as an instrument to spread rebellious plots. With that in mind, the High Chancellor created a system of hierarchal bishops and superior ministers to keep eye on Germany's religious institutions.

He pushed that paper aside to look at the ones underneath. He came across an envelope titled "German-American Relations Review." He opened it up. Inside he found many letters from Washington from Berlin in regards to German Tunisia's borders expanding into Afro-American territory. On another page, Washington warned Germany that expanding from French Guiana and into Suriname was a violation of their Monroe Doctrine and would result in invasion of their South American regions. Zeithen chuckled to himself. He was always amused that Americans had refused to acknowledge that they were no longer a superpower as of five hundred years ago but still acted as if they were. French Guiana, now New Germany, was about to take off into the anarchist regions of Alejandro Guamez' protectorate. Country by country, region by region, German forces would snake their way west into the occupied northern region of Brazil and then down along the Andes into Patagonia. The nations of United Colombia would fall like dominoes.

The only issue with the High Chancellor's South American campaign was that Portugal was no longer in his possession and therefore the German navies were stuck in the North Sea between England and Scandinavia. Zeithen had feared a Pacifican entrance in internal European affairs. Even though the late Pacifican Emperor's demise truly was accidental, the Empire would not listen to any rhetoric Germany had to offer. It was now the catalyst for Charles leading his mega navies and air forces across the Atlantic. Any further movement across the Alps would definitely result in the Anglo-Spanish coalition crossing the borders into France.

The High Chancellor tapped his chin with the envelope, pondering how to play his next moves. It was becoming more complicated than he had previously envisioned.

He heard someone tapping lightly on his door. "Ja, come in."

His secretary delicately walked in. "Heil Zeithen."

"Anja, you don't need to salute me each time you come in here. I see you at least forty times in a day. Now what is it?"

"I have excellent news, High Chancellor. This is just in from our leading scientists at the National Medical University of Berlin." She handed him a folder. "The Reichstag wants you to come to Charlottenburg Palace immediately."

Zeithen opened the folder and scanned over the information presented. Anja watched him pause and reread the same sentence a few times over. He looked stunned. "Oh my," he said.

"Isn't it wonderful, Chancellor?"

He closed the folder and put it under his arm. "It's more than wonderful, Anja." He smiled at her. "Have my escort ready to take me in five minutes."

"Yes, Chancellor." She hustled out of his office. He leaned back in his chair, holding the folder closely to his chest. It was the most wonderful news he had received in months. The sad irony of Anja's statement was that the reasons why she thought it was wonderful and his reasons behind why it was wonderful were completely different. And far more nefarious . . .

Warrenhari Zeithen hustled out of his escort vehicle toward Charlottenburg Palace, accompanied by some of the most elite units in all of Germany. He hurried past all the banners and statues and fountains towards the main lobby. Everyone inside saluted him but he was too elated to notice.

He and his units hurried into an eastern corridor where they entered a small presentation auditorium, where timid men it white lab coats waited anxiously for his arrival. They all saluted him as he sat down squarely in front of them.

"Gentlemen. I have received word that you have some excellent news for me today. Is that correct?"

"Yes, High Chancellor," said the head scientist, walking around a display holding a vial. "We at the National Medical University of Berlin have preformed countless tests on animals as well as a host people. We can with one hundred percent certainty say that we have indefinitely found the cure for the Human Immunodeficiency or AIDS Virus." Zeithen leaned forward in his chair. "What we have done is instead of using outside biological forces, have created a genetically adjusted form of the virus. It looks to make a host out of its own kind rather than foreign cells that make up the human body, causing the altered virus to commit cannibalism on a cellular level. HIV has been battling human antibodies for centuries but it is in no way prepared for an attack of the same entity."

"And this works?"

"Yes. All test subjects showed an improvement in health within two months. The trick is to catch it early enough. If subjects have had it for more than a few years then the virus has already manifested itself to greatly for the vaccine to have any real chance of helping."

"So should all citizens of the Reich receive this immediately?"

"No Chancellor. I'm suggesting though that all citizens be tested for the virus. A mandatory test would make sure everyone is accounted for, but giving uninfected people the vaccine would cause them to become ill with a type of hybrid virus. One that we don't have the cure for. As long as the original virus is present in the body, the vaccine will attack it and finish the job. But if administered to someone without the disease, the vaccine will simply look for the closest resembling host."

"How expensive is this to manufacture?"

"Not very much at all. The vaccine reproduces. We simply need to store it in the right environmental conditions that are optimum for viral reproduction." The scientist picked up the vial and handed it to Zeithen. He held it up to the light and gazed through it. The vaccine had an amber color to it. He then watched some of the monitors hanging from the ceiling, displaying microscopic videos taken of the vaccine in action. He looked back that the head scientist and extended the vial out back to him. The scientist grabbed hold of it but Zeithen wouldn't let go.

The High Chancellor looked him in the eye. "You will hand over the vaccine, its patents and all of yours and your team's research to the Ministry of the Interior's Medical Bureau immediately. As of now you are under the protection of the State. You may continue to be a faculty member of the university but you may not leave the Prefecture of Prussia. There are more terms and conditions that the Ministry of the Interior will give at a later point in time but these are the ones I wanted to give you personally. Just so that we are clear."

"I understand, Chancellor."

"Good." Warrenhari Zeithen let go of the vial and stood up. The units around the doors stood at attention. "You have done well, doctor. This is a great feat of achievement for Germany. You have made your Chancellor very proud and the Fatherland will not forget your services." He took the scientist's hand and shook it. "The Reich will reward you greatly. I would like to see you at dinner tonight, back here at Charlottenburg Palace. We can discuss the benefits and rewards of your team's work then."

"Thank you, Chancellor," said the doctor. Zeithen nodded his head. As he began to walk out of the assembly room, the scientists all saluted him.

"Heil Zeithen!"

The High Chancellor stood at the podium in front of the head legislative body and government officials of Germany in the Reichstag Central Ministry of the Interior. This is where Warrenhari Zeithen came to work everyday. This is where all national decisions were made, both domestic and foreign. Charlottenburg Palace was where most of the ministries and bureaus were located and the Executive Chancellery Office was simply where Zeithen's office was but this was the head building of the Reich. Banners hung down all around the central assembly room. Bright lights shined directly on him. Television screens hung in various places that showed a zoomed-in image of his face.

"Germans! Governors! Generals, representatives and ambassadors! The Reich has made a breakthrough today not only in medical advancement but also in the Glorious War. Our scientists are the brightest in the world. They have conquered plagues in the past and now they have conquered one of the vilest viruses in history. The Human Immunodeficiency Virus!"

The assembly began cheering and saluting as Zeithen held up one of the amber vials of the vaccine. "This vaccine, when administered early enough, can stop the virus from accelerating and eliminate it. Naturally, within the next few months, all citizens of Germany will be required to be tested for HIV in order to finally have a virus-free nation." The assembly again began to cheer and clap.

"But I have more good news." The assembly grew silent. "America wants this vaccine. A fifth of their population is infected with it the virus. Their own President of the R.N.A.

is infected with it. They also have been stifling our progress in North Africa. So what is Germany to do? Well, as we speak, Washington is getting the test results of our vaccine on medical test subjects. The whole world is receiving word of *our* breakthrough tonight! The whole world would love to have our German-made vaccine . . . but they can't have it."

The whole assembly was still hauntingly silent. "The only way they can get their miserable hands on it is if they can convince America to get out of Germany's way!" The audiences started to clap again. "They can out of our way in Libya and Suriname or let their population drop exponentially. They have a choice. They can choose their Monroe Doctrine or they can choose our vaccine." The assembly exploded with applause. "Either way, the Reich is victorious. This is our triumph! Either way, we win! *Germany wins!*"

END OF VOLUME I